STEALING HOME

BOOK 4

This book was donated by

Kristy Chou

Other Books in the
Spirit of the Game Series

Goal Line Stand (Book 1)
Full-Court Press (Book 2)
Second Wind (Book 3)
Three-Point Play (Book 5)
Cody's Varsity Rush (Book 6)

SPIRIT OF THE GAME

STEALING HOME

BOOK 4

BY TODD HAFER

zonderkidz

This book is dedicated to the life and memory
of Tim Hanson, a true athlete, a true friend.

A tip of my Yankees cap to Dave Dravecky and
T. J. McReynolds for their baseball insights.

The children's group of Zondervan

www.zonderkidz.com

Stealing Home
Copyright © 2004 by Todd Hafer

Requests for information should be addressed to:
Zonderkidz, Grand Rapids, Michigan 49530

ISBN: 0-310-70671-8

Library of Congress CIP Data applied for

Editor: Bruce Nuffer
Cover design Alan Close
Interior design: Susan Ambs
Art direction: Laura Maitner
Photos by Synergy Photographic
Printed in the United States of America

08 09 10 11 12 • 14 13 12 11 10 9 8 7 6

Contents

Prologue 9

1. Real Angels Throw Fastballs 15

2. The Showdown 33

3. High Heat 46

4. Scared to Death 59

5. Taking One for the Team 79

6. Danger in High Places 103

Epilogue 123

Foreword

I love sports. I have always loved sports. I have competed in various sports at various levels, right through college. And today, even though my official competitive days are behind me, you can still find me on the golf course, working on my game, or on a basketball court, playing a game of pick-up.

Sports have also helped me learn some of life's important lessons—lessons about humility, risk, dedication, teamwork, friendship. Cody Martin, the central character in "The Spirit of the Game" series, learns these lessons too. Some of them, the hard way. I think you'll enjoy following Cody in his athletic endeavors.

Like most of us, he doesn't win every game or every race. He's not the best athlete in his school, not by a long shot. But he does taste victory, because, as you'll see, he comes to understand that life's greatest victories aren't reflected on a scoreboard. They are the times when you rely on a strength beyond your own —a spiritual strength—to carry you through. They are the times when you put the needs of someone else before your own. They are the times when sports become a way to celebrate the life God has given you.

So read on, and may you always possess the true Spirit of the Game.

Toby McKeehan

Prologue

Excerpted from an interview in the *Grant Gazette,* weekly newspaper for Grant, Colorado:

Q: It must be a great way to end eighth grade, Cody, being named Grant Middle School's Most Courageous Athlete.

Well, I'm grateful for the award, but I don't think I deserve it. My best friend, Deke Porter, should have won. Pork Chop plays every game with more courage than anyone I've ever seen. He got my vote. I can't believe more people didn't vote for him. To tell you the truth, I didn't think I'd get a single vote.

Q: Aren't you selling yourself a bit short? After all, you led the football team to a historic upset—a shutout—of previously undefeated East, were named to the all-district tournament team in basketball, and placed at districts in distance running—all while coping with the loss of your mom.

It's weird hearing you list those things—it's hard to believe they all happened to me. But I give credit for it to God's grace and to the support of my coaches and a special group of friends—the ones I get to call teammates.

Q: You won a fair amount of games and races this past year, but you lost a lot, too. Do you ever cry when you lose?

I used to, but not anymore.

Q: How come?

I'll have to answer your question with one of my own. Have you ever watched someone die? It changes you forever. Don't get me wrong. I love winning. I hate losing—because it hurts so much. You put in all those hours of practice. Then it's game time, and you go all out every second. You can control the game right up to the final seconds. But then one little thing can make the difference between winning and losing. There's a very thin line between the two—one missed free throw, one holding penalty, swinging the bat a fraction of a second too late. One moment you think you're marching off with a championship trophy, and the next you're walking away with nothing but disappointment and pain.

But there's no thin line between life and death. They're a Grand Canyon apart. See, one minute my mom was in this world. She was breathing. She was so sick, but I could feel the life in her when I sat by her bedside and held her hand. But every day her breaths were getting weaker and farther apart. Then, on that afternoon ten months ago, the next breath just didn't come. She was gone. What was left was like a shell. It was her body but it wasn't her.

I hope that makes sense. At that moment, I grew up more in a few seconds than I had in my entire life. I learned that death is real and life is precious, and that a lost game is nothing to cry about. There are bigger things in life to cry about.

Q: Was your mom afraid when she knew she was dying?

Not at all—and that wasn't like her. She was afraid of all kinds of stuff. She feared spiders, snakes, and even loud thunder. And she was always afraid I would break my leg or my neck or something while I was playing my sports. But she didn't fear death at all. She used to look me in the eyes and say, "Cody, I am not afraid of this journey, because I know where it leads. I know."

She was so sure of heaven—of Jesus waiting for her, with arms open wide. My goal in life is to be that sure someday—to *know him the way she did. And I want to make her proud of me. And my sports are part of that. She came to all my games, ever since I was in T-ball, back before I started kindergarten. There's nothing like winning while your mom is in the stands cheering for you.*

Q: You dedicated this past sports year to your mom. Do you believe she can see you compete?

I do. I talk about this with Blake Randall, my youth pastor, all the time. I don't know if he totally agrees with me, but that's okay. I dedicated the season to Mom, and I was willing to knock down walls to win. I never cheated or talked smack or took cheap shots at anybody, but I brought the war every time. Because I believed Mom was watching, cheering for me just like always, and maybe grabbing an angel by the robe and yelling, "Did you see that? That's my son!"

So that's why I go as hard as I do. That's why I got the nickname Cody Crash in football. And even if Mom can't see me, maybe they have some kind of heavenly ESPN or something. Maybe she can at least get scores and highlights and commentary. Maybe she has some way of knowing that I'm out there representing every time, trying to make her proud, trying to make God proud. I still don't know if I've paid proper tribute to my mom. It feels like there's something left undone. But at least I know that I gave it my all—every single race, every single game. And that's the way it's always going to be.

Q: Speaking of games, do we even need to ask how you're going to spend your summer?

It will be all about baseball. Practice starts in about a month. I'm tired and my body is hurting right now. But once I see the Park and Rec guys mowing the infield over at Grant Field, building up the pitcher's mound, and laying down those snow-white chalk lines—Pork Chop says the chalk looks like powdered sugar—I'll be ready to slip on my mitt and play ball.

I don't know if I'll be able to play on August third, though. That will be the one-year anniversary of Mom's death. It's going to be a hard day for me. But I think my best chance to survive it will be out on the field.

Q: Do you plan to continue your athletic career in high school in the fall?

Oh, yeah. I can't wait. I don't know which teams I'll make—or if I'll make any team. But I'll be out there trying. I've been going to the Grant High games since I was a little kid. I've always dreamed of wearing the blue and silver. It will be heaven.

Q: Speaking of heaven, do you think there will be sports up there?

Dude, I can't imagine that it would be heaven without sports.

Chapter 1

Real Angels Throw Fastballs

Cody shielded his eyes with his right hand, his cinnamon-colored hair peeking out from under his ball cap, as he tracked the tiny sphere arcing against the midday Colorado sky. When it reached its zenith, he lost it for a moment. But then, as it dropped back toward earth, his eyes found it again. He slid to his right and waited. He risked a glance at Blake, who was staring at him in bewilderment.

He's wondering why I'm not moving under the ball, mitt up to catch it, Cody thought, laughing to himself. The ball was picking up speed now, looking as if it would thud on the grass to Cody's left. He stood, arms dangling at his sides, as the ball hurtled past his head.

Then, just as the ball was level with his hip, Cody crouched and stabbed his outfielder's mitt to the left—and snagged it only a foot from the ground.

"Had you worried, didn't I?" he said, chuckling.

Blake shook his head. "Nah, Code, I just thought you lost the ball in the sun."

Cody flipped the ball from his glove to his right hand. Then, with a flick of his wrist, he whipped a hard grounder to his youth pastor Blake. Blake dropped to his knees and scooped the ball into a well-worn softball mitt, his "church-league special," as he called it. Then he stood, rocked back, and fired a fast-ball that zoomed toward Cody's face.

Cody yawned. The ball bulleted toward him, less than ten feet from his nose now. He waited as long as he could and then snapped his glove hand up to his face, as if to swat a horsefly. The ball hit his glove with a deep smack.

"Yeow!" he yelled, letting the mitt slide off his hand, which he shook and flexed, curling and uncurling his fingers. "You had some mustard on that one, B!"

Blake flexed his right bicep. "Yeah, pretty good hose for a guy who plays only church-league softball, huh?"

Cody nodded. "Not bad. But watch this!" He went into an elaborate stretch. His eyes bored into Blake.

He shook off two signals from an imaginary catcher, then planted his left foot and brought his arm forward like a bullwhip.

He tried to reign in a smile when he heard the pop of the ball in Blake's mitt less than two seconds later.

"You know," Blake said as he bounced a bumpy grounder toward Cody, "biblical legend has it that some angels did this with the stone used to seal Jesus' tomb—after the Resurrection."

Cody cocked his head. "You're kidding, right? Angels played baseball? The only baseball-playing angels I've heard of are the ones in Anaheim."

Blake nodded. "Well, some people believe different. I know it sounds far-fetched, but think about it. That huge stone weighed about two thousand pounds—as much as your dad's car. It would have taken a bunch of guys with levers to move it into a groove in the bedrock of the tomb.

"Then it was sealed with wax, and that signified that a burial was final. Whoever was inside the tomb wasn't going anywhere."

Cody squinted against the sun as he sidearmed the ball toward Blake. "B," he said, "do *you* believe that legend, or whatever it is?"

Blake grinned and pitched the ball back to Cody. "You know, I kinda do. I mean, think about it. Jesus came to life—after two days inside a dark tomb.

Maybe he pushed that huge stone out of the way himself, or maybe the angels did it. In either case, those angels had to be amped. And what better way to celebrate than toss around the very stone that was supposed to be massive enough to seal their Lord's eternal fate?"

"You have a point." Cody fired the ball again. "Do you think the angels could throw a banana curveball like that one?"

Blake caught the toss. He hesitated for a moment, then plucked the ball from his mitt, tossing it up and down in his right hand as if it were an egg that was too hot to handle. "I'm sure they could," he said, "but I have a feeling they didn't. Think about it. Your Lord and Master has just defeated death itself, and you're standing there at ground zero, toying with the boulder that was supposed to imprison him forever. Nah, I think in that case, you gotta throw the high, hard cheese. Like this!"

With that, Blake ripped a fastball that nearly tore the mitt off Cody's hand. "Nice grab, dude," he said. "I'd say you're ready for baseball season."

Cody removed his faded Red Sox cap and dabbed sweat from his forehead with his T-shirt sleeve. "I hope so," he said. "I just hope we don't have to play any team called the Angels!"

Coach Lathrop was a small wiry man with the hairiest arms Cody had ever seen. With his pushed-in nose and stiff, military-style buzz cut, he seemed more like a wrestling coach than a baseball coach, but this was his second summer at the helm of the Rockies, the US Baseball League team for the city of Grant, after three years with a USBL team up in Boulder, Colorado. Before that, he had coached high school ball back in Indiana or Illinois; Cody couldn't remember which.

"Okay," Coach Lathrop was saying to the thirteen eighth- and ninth-graders-to-be half-circled around him, "it's good to see so many familiar faces back this year. And I'm guessing most of you have met our newest Rockie, right?"

Cody nodded at AJ Murphy, who had transferred to Grant Middle School early in the spring. Murphy had made a name for himself in PE class, always getting extra-base hits in softball games. Sure, the PE games were slow-pitch, and anybody could get wood on a softball, which was as big as a grapefruit. Still, Murphy had a sturdy build and a smooth swing, and Cody couldn't wait to see how far he could hit a baseball—*if* he could hit a baseball.

"Murphy," Coach Lathrop was saying now, "I know you played ball on a tournament team up in Denver last summer. What's your position?"

Murphy smacked his fist into his glove and smashed a clod of dirt under his toe. "Mostly third base, Coach," he said, his face expressionless. "Some center field, too. But I'll play wherever you need me."

Murphy glanced nervously at Cody, who gave him a reassuring nod. During PE class, the two of them had talked about baseball, and Cody revealed that he was thinking about playing third. But as baseball season drew closer, he determined he would play center field, his position since T-ball. After a long year of football, basketball, and track, he had no desire to field screaming line drives or have base runners charging toward him.

"Turns out," Coach Lathrop said, "we may need someone to play the hot corner. Our third baseman from last year, Matt Slaven, has taken to tennis this summer." By the way Coach Lathrop said *tennis*, Cody could tell he wasn't a fan of the game.

The man says tennis *the way I say* algebra, he thought.

Coach Lathrop went on about how he had never won a game in a post-season tournament in all his years of coaching baseball. He concluded his speech by vowing, "This year that's going to change."

Then he told the team to take four laps around the field before drills began.

Cody settled in next to Murphy as they trotted around the diamond across from Grant Memorial Park. "Welcome to the team," he said. "We really need a new third baseman."

Murphy looked over at him. "Thanks. I'm glad you decided to move to the outfield. I wouldn't want to play out there—not fast enough. So, you think the coach is right about the postseason? We have a chance to do something this summer?"

"Maybe. It's a tough league, especially the team from Lincoln. They're a free-swinging, base-stealing bunch. And they've got this pitcher, Madison, who I hear is throwing in the mid-seventies already. He threw a two-hitter against us last year. It was brutal. It was like trying to hit an aspirin speeding over the plate. When I face him this year, I think I'll just close my eyes, pray, and swing."

Murphy whistled grimly through his teeth. "I hear ya. That guy sounds like he's got serious gas. I hope he's got at least some control, though. I'd hate to get hit with a seventy-five-mile-an-hour heater. That would do some damage. Last year our pitcher, this big dude named Miller, he hit a guy in the face and broke his orbital bone. And Miller can't throw in the seventies, not by a long shot."

Cody shook his head. "Well, they call Madison 'Madman', because control isn't exactly his strong suit. But maybe it will be better this season."

"I hope so. Man, mid-seventies—that's flat out scary. The batting cages I practice in have pitching machines that go up to seventy. When I crank 'em up that high, it's all I can do not to run away when those blazers start coming at me."

After laps, the Rockies paired off to play catch and loosen up their arms. As he watched some of his teammates send throws into the dirt—or sailing over their partners' heads—Cody was glad he had spent so much time practicing with Blake and going on morning runs with Drew Phelps, Grant Middle School's distance-running legend. He hadn't lost any fitness since school ended. His right arm felt loose and strong. And after a long sports season, it was good to be in baseball mode again. The game was more relaxed. The crowds were smaller, and there wasn't the pressure of representing your school.

Since Cody had run with Murphy, he felt it would be okay to partner up with Pork Chop to work on throwing.

Let somebody else babysit the new guy for a while, he reasoned. *Besides, there's something strange about Murphy. He never smiles. I get this weird vibe off him.*

Pork Chop obviously hadn't thrown a baseball in a while. His tosses were all over the place. But that wouldn't matter. Chop played first base, so he wouldn't be asked to gun down too many base runners. His main job on defense was to snare ground balls or hard liners up the right field line, and make himself a big and sure target for putouts at first. And at five eleven and two hundred pounds, he was quite a target.

Cody studied his friend. Sweat was already trickling down the coffee-and-cream skin of his forehead. Chop still carried extra weight in his stomach, as if he were hiding a throw pillow under his T-shirt. But his shoulders and biceps already seemed larger and more defined than they were when school ended. The work on the family farm and the weight lifting sessions with his big brother, Doug, who was headed to the University of Colorado on a football scholarship, were paying off.

Now, Cody thought, as he watched an errant throw sail three feet over his head, *if only Chop could get all that strength under control!*

"Chop," he said, laughing, "any chance you'll actually throw a ball to me? This isn't keep-away, you know. Not fetch either."

"I meant to throw that one high," Pork Chop said. "Wanted to see if your vertical has improved any. But it looks like you still have no hops."

"Yeah, right. Yao Ming couldn't have caught that one."

It didn't take long for the Rockies to round into a strong team. During the last practice before the season opener, Cody marveled as he watched Pork Chop stretch to backhand a screamer of a line drive, off the bat of Terry Alston, who had been Grant Middle School's best all-around athlete. "Chop's like a vacuum at first," he whispered to himself. "He snarfs up anything that comes near him."

Later in the practice, Alston produced a "web gem" of his own—in an effort, no doubt, to upstage his arch rival, Pork Chop. With Coach Lathrop hitting fly balls to the outfield, Alston sprinted from the warning track, straw-colored hair flying, to shallow right field, then dove on his stomach and slid to snare the fly, capturing it in the top of his webbing. A few of the Rockies hooted in approval. "Alston's got himself an ice-cream-cone catch," hollered Murphy. Pork Chop turned to Alston and raised his mitt to his forehead in salute.

Cody couldn't rein in his smile on the ride home. He wondered if his dad would ask him what was behind the smile, but Luke Martin was so focused on the road that Cody figured he could be on fire and his dad wouldn't notice.

But if his dad had asked him, Cody would have told him that he was smiling because the team was looking tough. With Alston and Greg Gannon flanking him in the outfield, Cody felt confident that the trio could chase down any ball hit to them.

The infield was solid, too. Chop was a rock at first, and Gage McClintock, a reliable middle-distance runner on the track team, was also a dependable second baseman. And at the hot corner, AJ Murphy was fearless, with a cannon for an arm.

Bart Evans played shortstop when he wasn't pitching, and he wasn't a great fielder. But if he was able to secure the ball, he could throw out a first base-bound runner from almost any position, including from his knees—or even the seat of his pants.

Mark Goddard, who played every sport without mastering any of them, was catcher—mainly because no one else wanted to wear the heavy gear during the summer's heat. Still, Goddard didn't let many pitches get by him, even when Bart Evans—or his twin brother and fellow pitcher, Brett—tossed one in the dirt. Most importantly, Goddard wasn't afraid to guard the plate as a runner charged home from third.

We could actually do some damage, Cody thought. *Maybe we'll even win a tournament or two.*

In the season opener, the Rockies faced the Braves, a strong team from Pueblo, which was seventy-five miles southwest of Grant. Cody remembered them from last year, when they beat Grant by two or three runs. They weren't a great hitting team, but they had Guzman, a hard-throwing right-hander almost as big as Pork Chop. He couldn't throw fire like Madison, but he had a tireless arm. He had gone the full seven innings last year, and Chop and the Evans twins had been the only guys to earn a hit off him.

As the Rockies went through pregame stretches and drills, Cody's mind started to wander. Almost out of instinct, he kept looking to the ancient stands behind the backstop, searching for his mother's face.

He took a deep breath and then returned to tossing the ball with Pork Chop. After a few throws, Chop held the ball in his huge first baseman's mitt, staring at it as if it were a still life apple in a painting, and then looked at Cody.

Cody could feel his friend's eyes studying him. "Code, what's wrong, dawg?" he said finally.

"What makes you think anything's wrong?"

You're throwing like an old washwoman. Something's gotta be eatin' you. I mean, usually you wing it pretty good, for a skinny white boy, anyway. So what's up? A week ago you were all amped for the season to start. And now—"

Cody shook his head slowly. "Something just hit me, Chop. See, I started thinking about this time last year—the beginning of baseball season. Mom was pretty sick by then, but she made it to our first couple games, remember? This is the last sport she saw me play."

Pork Chop's head drooped. "Ah, I'm sorry. I'm sorry about doggin' you about your throws. I shoulda known, shoulda remembered. You gonna be okay?"

"I think so," Cody said, his voice crumbling around the edges.

Cody was relieved when Coach Lathrop called the team to the dugout to announce the batting order. He hoped that once the game began, he could shed the sadness that weighed on him, just as he had shed his down-filled coat last winter whenever he entered his overheated house, where his dad had kept the thermostat at a nausea-inducing seventy-five degrees.

"Martin," Coach Lathrop said without looking at him, "you're leading off. We need someone who can get the bat on the ball every time, and you've been making good contact lately. Alston, you bat second. Evans, Brett-type, you're third. And there's no mystery about our cleanup man, is there?"

Pork Chop flexed his right bicep and gazed at it with admiration. "Just get on base, y'all, and I'll bring everybody home."

"Don't get too cocky, Mr. Porter," Coach Lathrop warned. "This Guzman's got pretty good stuff."

Pork Chop smiled. "So do I, Coach."

The Braves were up first, and Brett set them down in order—via a strikeout and two weak infield grounders.

Cody stared grimly at Guzman as he stepped into the batter's box and assumed his stance. *Well*, he reasoned, *at least I know what's coming. Okay, Guz, bring the heat.*

Guzman's first pitch painted the outside corner for a called strike.

"It's okay," Cody heard Chop shout from the dugout. "Wait for your pitch."

Cody tapped his bat twice on home plate as Guzman loaded up for pitch number two. *As hard as this guy is throwing*, he told himself, *if I can just make contact, I'll probably get a hit.*

The pitch came, and Cody did make contact, but not with his bat. Guzman threw low and inside, smacking Cody on his left shin. He didn't know if it was the pain or the sheer force of the impact that knocked him down, but there he was, on his back, embarrassed and staring up at a cloudless sky.

"You okay, young man?" he heard the umpire ask.

"Yeah," he answered, climbing tentatively to his feet. He put some weight on his leg and said a silent prayer of thanks when it didn't buckle under him. But it hurt, like someone had whacked his shin with a hammer. He limped his way to first base.

He saw Coach Lathrop signal for a time-out and trot to the bag. "That guy's got a wicked-hard fastball," the coach observed.

"Yeah. Can't wait to see the bruise," Cody said, trying to sound nonchalant.

"You need to come out of the game?"

"Nah, I'm fine. It's feeling better already."

"You sure? I don't want you in here if you can't run the bases."

Oh, silly me, Cody thought. *I thought you might be concerned about my leg.* "Really, Coach," he said. "I'm good."

Coach Lathrop rubbed his chin, his hand making a scratchy sound on the thick, half-inch red-and-gray stubble, then proclaimed, "All right, then. I'm leaving you in. Be glad it wasn't Madison who just plunked you. He'd have snapped your shinbone like a toothpick."

As the coach jogged back to the dugout, Cody peeled off his batting glove and shoved it in the back pocket of his pants.

Alston was at the plate now, his favorite green aluminum bat on his shoulder. He swung at Guzman's first offering and hit a weak dribbler right back to the mound. Guzman scooped up the gift grounder, turned

to second, and threw Cody out easily. Then the second baseman rifled the ball to first. Alston, apparently
angry with himself for the poor effort, didn't run hard,
and the Braves turned one of the easiest double plays
Cody had even seen.

Brett Evans whiffed on three straight pitches, and
the first inning ended in a 0–0 deadlock.

The Braves picked up a run in their half of the
second, as Guzman hit a two-out double that resulted
in the game's first score.

Pork Chop led off the bottom of the second. He
ignored two pitches at his knees and then fouled a
high fastball straight into the backstop.

Guzman tried to confuse Pork Chop on the next
pitch, throwing his first changeup of the game.

But the Rockies' first baseman was ready. He waited
on the pitch and then drove it over the fence in
straightaway center field. Guzman could only turn and
watch his chances for a shutout sail out of the park.

Cody thought Chop would be smiling as he rounded
the bases, but his friend's expression was grim.

Guzman set the rest of the Rockies down in order,
and as the team took the field, Cody saw Chop grab
Alston's arm. "We should have three runs right now,
Hollywood, not just one. We should be winning. But
you have to go and swing on the first pitch, just like

you did all the time last year—if you can call that a swing. I've seen rusty gates swing better. And then you jog to first like you got arthritis? That was weak!"

Alston pulled away from the bigger player and stared at him, eyes burning. "You best back off, fat boy. I've had about a gutful of you. Why don't you take your black—" Cody felt his heart race. The last guy who hurled a racial slur at Pork Chop, a tall but skinny kid at the mall earlier in the summer, lost consciousness—and two teeth. "Say 'hey' to your dentist for me," Pork Chop had said before walking away from his fallen opponent.

Now Chop was smiling at Alston, but it was the kind of smile that always frightened Cody. "My black *what*, Alston? Which part of my blackness do you want me to take somewhere? It's important to be specific—we learned that in composition, remember?"

Before Alston could answer, Coach Lathrop was on them. "Is this baseball or debate, gentlemen? Because if you want to yap, you're wearing the wrong uniforms."

"Sorry, Coach," Alston said. "Porter was just criticizing me, and I was defending myself."

Coach Lathrop turned on Pork Chop. "I'm the coach here, Porter. Don't forget it. I don't care how big you are or who your brother is. Got it?"

"Yes, Coach."

Coach Lathrop headed for the dugout. As they jogged to their positions at first base and right field, Pork Chop hissed to Alston, "After the game—in the park. It's on."

"Finally," Alston shot back. "I can't wait."

Chapter 2

The Show- down

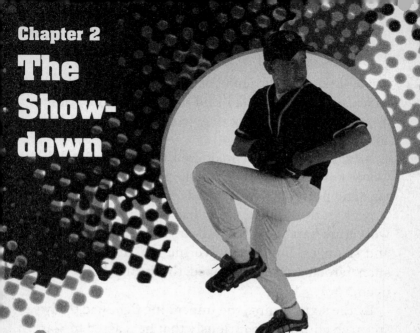

Cody stood in center field, praying fervently. *Please, God,* he pleaded, *don't let them fight. I have to admit, I have been hoping all year that they would. I'm just as curious as everybody else about who would win. But now that it's going to happen, it just makes me sick to my stomach.*

Cody watched as Pork Chop snagged a bullet line drive up the first base line for the first out of the inning. His friend was huge. He could probably take Alston. But Alston was lightning-fast. He was mean— and a year older than the other freshman-to-be, thanks to his dad sending him to a private school for the first of his two years in eighth grade.

"What a twisted sense of priorities some parents have," Cody's mom had said of the decision. "Some people will do anything to give their kids an athletic advantage."

Advantage. Cody considered the word. But who would have the advantage if Chop and Alston fought? Size and power—or speed and cunning?

Back in third grade, Cody had read an account of a wolverine battling a black bear. The bear was bigger and stronger, but the wolverine had attacked with such ferocity that he ripped the bear's belly wide open.

By the sixth inning, the impending fight had Cody's stomach churning so furiously that he reacted too late to a lazy fly ball to shallow center field, and it dropped in for a base hit. He could hear Coach Lathrop screaming at him from the dugout steps, but he couldn't decipher what he was saying.

When the game ended in a 4–1 Rockies loss, Cody decided to find a quiet spot to talk Chop out of the brawl. He saw Chop and Alston arguing conspiratorially between home plate and the backstop, and headed in their direction.

Then Coach Lathrop stepped into his path. "Martin," he said through near-clenched teeth, "don't ever let me see you fall asleep in the outfield again. You hear me?"

"Yes sir," Cody said robotically, angling his body to steal a peek around him to see if Chop and Alston were still jawing.

"Good. I'm glad we understand each other. Now, go bag up the bats and put them in the back of my truck."

Cody felt a wave of panic wash over him. "But, Coach—"

"But what, Martin? You too good to help with cleanup? I thought you church boys were supposed to help out all the time."

Cheap shot, Cody thought angrily. "I'll be happy to help," he said cheerfully.

He sprinted to the dugout, collected the bats, and stuffed them into the dirty white canvas bag that he figured Coach Lathrop must have been using since the 1980s. He slung the bag over his shoulder and jogged to find the coach's truck.

"Chop," he whispered to no one in particular, "please don't do this. Or at least just trash-talk for a while until I can find you."

Cody flipped the bag into the bed of the truck and then sprinted for the park. He checked the tennis courts first but found only a pair of squirrels chasing each other along one of the nets.

"The pool," he said. "They must be at the pool."

The park's swimming pool hadn't been filled this summer, due to cracks around its base and problems with the filtration system. Two high school guys had fought there earlier in the summer. The battle had drawn such a crowd that the police showed up.

When he saw the entire baseball team gathered around the perimeter of the deep end, Cody knew he had found the battle site. A few grade-schoolers on bikes were parked along the opposite end, their front wheels almost ready to slip over the edge.

As Cody climbed down the rickety aluminum ladder at the shallow end of the pool, he offered one of his favorite prayers—*Help!*

He made his way into the deep end, where Chop and Alston circled each other warily, the latter firing a few jabs in an effort to keep his bigger opponent at bay. When Chop took two steps back to avoid being tagged with a punch, Cody stepped between them, the two best athletes and fiercest competitors in the school.

This is a fine spot, he thought, *right between the bear and the wolverine. I must be crazy.*

"What are you, Martin," Alston spat, "our referee?"

"Dawg," Chop said grimly, "you best step off now. I mean it. Don't get in the middle of this."

Cody swallowed hard. "I'm not here to referee. I'm just here to say something to the two biggest idiots, the two most selfish morons, in the whole town."

Alston's face puckered and twitched, as if he'd just bitten into a lemon. "Wuh–what?!"

"You heard me, Alston," Cody said, hoping no one could hear the fear that constricted his throat. "You know, the way you finished strong in basketball this year, the way you ran track—I thought you were maturing. I guess I was wrong."

Cody could tell Alston was forming a response, but he turned his back on him and faced Pork Chop. "And you, you're our team captain. Is this what captains do—beat down their teammates?"

Pork Chop glared at Cody, who spun around and took two steps back so he could see both of his teammates. "You know, I was talking to your brother a couple days ago, Chop. He said our class might be the best crop of freshmen athletes ever to hit the high school. He says we have a chance to take state in football and basketball, maybe track, too."

Pork Chop nodded in agreement but his expression didn't change. And Alston looked like he was ready to pounce on Cody, perhaps to give him a warm-up pummeling before the main event.

Cody inhaled deeply. "You guys are the best athletes in this whole region—maybe even the whole state. Just think what you could accomplish if you actually worked together." He looked toward Alston.

"Your speed and skill." He nodded at Chop. "And your size, power, and guts."

"Look—," Alston began.

"No, you look," Cody interrupted. "I'm sick of both of you, trash-talking for a whole year, tearing each other down, bringing your teams down. You know, a team divided against itself is never going to win much. But if you're that selfish, go ahead. Beat each other to a pulp. Prove your manhood. Show those grade-schoolers down at the shallow end how team leaders solve their problems. Be their role models. But I'm not going to stay around to watch. I'm *so* outta here."

Cody glanced up and wagged his head sadly at the Rockies who had gathered to watch. "You guys here to see blood, huh? Good. I hope you get what you want." He went back to the ladder and climbed out.

"Cody," he heard someone call as he marched away, "wait up." He turned to see Murphy jogging after him.

Cody gave the new guy an approving smile. "Well, at least one of our players has some common sense."

"Yeah, I guess so. Dude, what you did back there? That was *cool*."

"Apparently, you're the only one who thinks so. Everyone else is staying to watch the carnage."

"No, that girl walked away, too."

Cody felt his jaw drop. "Girl? I didn't see any girl."

"Yeah, she was standing in back of all those kids on their bikes. A real fly honey, with glasses. I think she's in our grade."

"Robyn," the word flopped out of Cody's mouth before he could reel it back in.

"Yeah, that's right, Robyn. She a . . . uh . . . friend of yours?"

Cody shook his head wearily. "Yeah," he sighed, "I guess so."

"I take it you don't want to talk about it."

"You take it correctly."

"Oh. Well, you wanna head back over to the diamond? I was terrible at the plate today. You think you could pitch me a few so I can work on my swing?"

Cody sandwiched his head between his hands for a moment. "You know what, Murph? Let's do it another time, okay? I'm kinda tired and stressed, and I think I need to go home and have a nervous breakdown now."

After Murph shrugged and headed back to the diamond, Cody felt the pull, like that of an electromagnet, trying to draw him back to the park. But he knew he couldn't go. "You make an exit speech like that," he whispered to himself, "you gotta *stay* exited." He slid off his baseball cleats, pulled on his running shoes, and began a slow trot home.

There was a note taped to the front door when he arrived. It was written in Beth's loopy cursive hand, which Cody thought looked like a sixth grader's penmanship.

> *Dear Cody,*
>
> *Sorry we missed your game. We hit heavy traffic on the way back from our lunch date in Denver. Super sorry about that. We've gone for a walk. Look forward to hearing about the big game when we get back.*

"Yeah," Cody muttered sarcastically, "I bet you look forward to it." Sure, Beth *would* ask about the game. She was good about that—always asking him how his workouts were going, which sports he planned to play in high school. But he wasn't sure why she was asking. Was she really interested, or was she just trying to get him to accept her as his dad's girlfriend—and the person who might someday be his step—he couldn't even allow himself to think the word, much less say it.

"The world is officially nuts," he said, searching the refrigerator for a snack. "I'm almost fourteen and a half years old and I don't have a girlfriend. My dad's forty-two and he *does*. I think I'm gonna be sick."

He slung his body across the couch and tried to find something worth watching on television. A bowling tournament was the most interesting thing he could find. "Scary," he said.

Through the epic fifth frame of the tournament, Cody battled the urge to call Pork Chop. *Let him call me,* he huffed to himself. *I can't believe he didn't just walk away with me. What does he have to lose? Everyone at school knows he's the man. Still, if he got hurt—*

Before the sixth frame ended, the urge beat Cody. He dialed the Porter house and got a busy signal. He hit the redial button ten times, with the same result.

He had begun to pace the living room when the phone rang. He almost dove on it like it was a fumble in the end zone. He was surprised that, when he heard Robyn's voice on the other end of the line, he wasn't disappointed—much.

"Hey, Hart," he said. "I gotta know—did you hear anything about the fight? I heard you walked away."

"Well," she said, her voice like cotton candy, "I started to, but then I went back. I had to, you know, so someone could tell you if your speech worked. And by the way, it was awesome, Cody. I'm so proud of you."

"Thanks, Hart," he said. "You know, I kind of owe it all to you. Remember how you stood up for Greta this past year, when everybody was doggin' her in the halls at school? I guess I figured that if you could do it, so could I. You kinda inspired me, or something. Besides, if I hadn't stepped in, you probably would have, huh?"

"Are you crazy? Get between Alston and Porter when they're both in a macho rage? I like my face just the way it is, thank you very much."

"So do I." Cody regretted the words as soon as they tumbled from his lips.

"What a nice thing to say, Cody. Thanks!"

"Anyway, Hart," he added quickly, "what happened? Did they end up fighting? I mean, I've called Chop, like, a hundred times, and—"

"Cody." Robyn's voice was still feather soft, but there was authority in it. There was weight to it. It reminded him of his mother's voice. "You need to chill," she said. "There was no fight."

"Really? That's great! But how?"

"I'll tell you how. After you left, Chop and Alston are just standing there, like two macho idiots. Finally, Alston says, 'You gonna do something, Porter, then do it. I'm not gonna stand here all night.'

"Then Porter, clever dude that he is, replies, 'Why don't *you* do something?' This is followed by more staring and glaring. A few of the kids on bikes shake their heads and pedal away. Your friend Mr. Porter looks desperately uncomfortable. But I know he's not going to back down. So I walk down toward the deep end, and I tell him I need to talk to him about something. I figure that way, I can step in without really stepping in, you know?"

"Yeah."

"Anyway, Pork Chop starts backing off. But he's still yapping as he's moving. 'No way is this over,' he tells Alston.

"Alston says, 'You got that right. You get back in my face, and I'm crackin' your oversize skull!'

"'Don't you mean my oversize *black* skull?' Chop asks. And the tension is as thick as tar. Something comes over Alston. He actually looks ashamed, or at least embarrassed. He looks like he wants to squirm out of his own skin, like one of those snakes on the Discovery Channel.

"Everything is all quiet for a minute or so. Then Alston looks down and says, 'Look, what I said before —I shouldn't have said that, okay? I don't know where that came from. I'm not a racist or anything. I don't roll like that.'"

Cody whistled through his teeth. "Whoa! Alston said that? That's almost like an apology. That would be two apologies from him in the same year! I can't believe it."

"I don't think Chop could believe it, either. Now it's his turn to look like he's been stun gunned. He's shaking his head and frowning, like he's concentrating on something really important to him."

"Like dinner."

"Ha ha ha. So anyway, Chop finally shrugs his shoulders and says, 'Okay, TA, but this doesn't change the beating I'm gonna put on you someday.'

"'Yeah, right,' Alston says. 'We'll see.' Before Chop can retort, the Evans twins, God bless 'em, they drag him out of the pool before his mouth ends the truce."

"I am so relieved, Hart. I was praying that no blood would get spilled in the pool."

"I guess Chop's guardian angels were working overtime. Hey, Code, what is it about you guys and your man-egos, anyway?"

"I have no idea. I'm fresh outta answers on that one."

"Well, try this question, then. I have to know—how did you find the strength to walk away? It must have been so hard not to stick around and see what would happen, especially with your best friend involved."

Cody laughed sadly. "Yeah, it was. But, on the other hand, I was so disgusted about the whole thing. And I didn't want to see Chop get hurt. I'm not saying Alston could take him, but he is older than the rest of us. And he gets in lots of fights. Chop almost never does. He doesn't have to. He just flexes those biceps, puffs out his chest, and that's enough to strike terror in most people's hearts."

Cody heard a click on the line. "Uh," Robyn said, a hint of apology in her voice, "that's the other line, and I better take it. My mom's supposed to be calling."

"That's cool, Hart. I'll see you around. And thanks again for what you did today."

"You did the hard part. Till whenever, then—"

Chapter 3

High Heat

Cody called the Porter house
five more times over the weekend,
leaving messages for Pork Chop each time.

On Monday afternoon Pork Chop's brother dropped
him off for practice, and Cody walked purposefully to
his friend.

"Hey, Code," Chop said with a forced laugh. "How
you livin'?"

"I don't know, Chop. How's your answering
machine—still working?"

"Look, dawg, I'm sorry, okay? I know you called me
a bunch, and I shoulda hit you back. I just had a lot of
thinking to do this weekend."

Cody leveled his eyes on Chop. "You get anything sorted out?"

"I'm not sure. I'm trying to figure out who to be mad at—who needs to get rocked."

Cody sighed. "Maybe nobody does. Maybe we all just need to focus on the sport at hand. Maybe some of us could focus on being teammates instead of enemies."

Pork Chop gave a noncommittal nod. "Maybe. We do have the Plainsmen coming up this weekend. Those guys are tough."

Cody watched Alston and Chop carefully through the week's practices. They didn't speak much, but that was okay, because that meant no trash-talking. He felt nervousness buzzing in his stomach during Wednesday's practice, when Alston and Chop found themselves throwing to each other.

The tosses got progressively harder, as each tried to force a yelp of pain—or at least a wince or grimace— out of the other. But both remained stone-faced, even though their throws were hitting the respective mitts with the angriest smacks and pops Cody had ever heard—at least since the Rockies faced Madison the previous season.

The Plainsmen were a collection of players from a handful of tiny towns, like Grant, that dotted

Colorado's eastern plains. They were always one of the toughest teams in the USBL, and they usually won their share of trophies at various independent tournaments. Not surprisingly, the Plainsmen came to the Grant baseball and softball complex riding a five-game winning streak, including a first-place finish at a big three-day tournament in Kansas.

After five innings, it appeared the streak was due to be snapped. Grant held a 3–1 lead, and Bart Evans hadn't allowed a base hit since the first inning. Meanwhile, Alston had two doubles, and Pork Chop had launched his second homer of the season, a towering shot to right field. Cody was the first person out of the dugout to congratulate him as he trotted home and jumped on the plate with both feet.

Cody led off the bottom of the sixth, still hoping for his first base hit of the young season. *Coach Lathrop's going to pull me from the leadoff spot if I go hitless this game,* he scolded himself as he assumed his stance.

Harris, the Plainsmen hurler, was lanky and had a herky-jerky delivery that made it hard for Cody to time his pitches. He had struck out swinging on his first two trips to the plate—then hit a high pop-up that the Plainsmen catcher barely had to move to catch.

Come on, Harris, Cody thought, *just give me one pitch I can hit, since my dad's here to watch me.*

Harris's first offering was an ankle-high fastball that Cody nearly swung at. He was way out in front of the second pitch, swinging so hard that he felt he might corkscrew himself into the ground.

He saw Harris smirk as he snagged the throw from his catcher. Cody wanted to charge the mound and force-feed the baseball to the pitcher. *Oh, Harris,* he thought, *I'd love to see you try that smirk with a mouthful of horsehide.*

Harris's third pitch was a fastball right down the middle of the plate. Cody was so enthralled with the image of mashing a baseball into Harris's mouth that he didn't even have time to think about swinging.

Harris shook his head, as if amused by the whole situation.

Cody took a deep breath as he stepped out of the batter's box to collect himself.

Dear God, he prayed silently, *help me to get a grip on my temper. I know that self-control is part of the fruit of the Spirit. Apparently, for me, that part of the fruit isn't ripe yet.*

"He's got a little hitch in his delivery. Don't get fooled by that," Cody heard a voice say. "You wait for your pitch. Be patient, dude!"

Whose voice is that? Cody wondered as he stepped back into the batter's box. Then it hit him. The voice belonged to Beth. *Great,* he thought, *now my dad's girl-friend is giving me hitting advice.*

He watched Harris go into his windup. He tightened his grip on his bat. Harris began to bring his soda-straw right arm forward. Then, as if posing for a quick photo opportunity, he stopped his motion for just a moment.

Well, how about that, Cody thought as he studied the fastball coming toward him, belt high. *He does have a hitch in his delivery.*

Cody felt the loud metallic click when the sweet spot of his bat met Harris's pitch. The Plainsmen center fielder was playing Cody too shallow, and he had no chance to field the bullet line drive that caromed off the fence in straightaway center field—275 feet from home plate.

Cody made a wide turn at first, then hustled back to the bag when the Plainsmen's second baseman cut off the throw from the outfield. He risked a glance to the bleachers behind home plate and saw Beth pumping her fist in the air and nodding approvingly, like a black-haired bobble-head doll.

Cody allowed himself a small smile as he took his lead from first.

Okay, Lord, he prayed, *I just got my first hit of the season, thanks to advice from a girl. I guess the Bible wasn't kidding when it says you work in mysterious ways.*

Alston followed Cody with a strong at bat. With the count at 3–2, he fouled off four straight fastballs before a frustrated Harris missed with a slider, giving the Rockies base runners on first and second.

Brett Evans swung on his first pitch, an inside fastball just above his hands. Harris fielded the resulting weak come-backer to the mound, then turned and threw to second in time to put out a hard-sliding Alston. And the second baseman, leaping to avoid Alston's cleats, fired a frozen rope to first to nail Evans by half a step.

Cody made it to third on the play, but he knew his team had missed a chance to blow the game wide open.

Harris, realizing his team had dodged a bullet, carefully painted the inside corners of the strike zone throughout Pork Chop's at bat. With the count at 2–2, Chop tried to muscle a pitch over the fence in right, but the Plainsmen fielder snared it on the warning track, giving the visitors a chance for a final-inning victory.

Bart Evans struck out the first batter he faced, but then issued two walks. Harris helped his own cause with a double to the gap in left center, tying the score at 3–3. Harris then stole third on an Evans changeup to the Plainsmen catcher.

Bart bore down and struck out the catcher, bringing up the shortstop.

This should be an easy out, Cody thought. *Their shortstop looks like he's about twelve. I don't think he's gotten the bat off his shoulder all afternoon.*

"Come on, Milo," Cody heard the Plainsmen coach bellow. "Be a big stick out there, boy!"

"I'd much prefer it if you'd be a little stick, Milo," Cody whispered. "How about a carrot stick? Or a matchstick? Come on, Milo. We need another win. How 'bout throwing us a bone, okay?"

Milo stood statue-like as two Bart Evans curveballs looped in for called strikes.

"That's it, Bart," Cody muttered. "Throw this stiff one more hook, and we're in business."

Evans did go to his curve again, but Milo was ready. He chopped down at the ball, like a little child swatting a bee. The ball nose-dived to the infield grass and then began rolling, as if in slow motion, toward the left of the pitcher's mound.

Bart's momentum had taken him away from the direction of the hit, but he quickly gathered himself and veered toward the ball. Murphy, however, was charging in from short. "Mine!" he yelled. Bart obediently stopped.

Murphy sprinted toward the ball. Cody could tell he was going to bare-hand it and fire it to Chop.

Milo was dashing to first base, but it looked like Murphy would make the play.

Until, that is, he overran the ball and came up with nothing but a handful of air—and a few blades of grass. Harris loped in to score.

The Rockies got the next batter out but were unable to overcome the visitors' momentum in the bottom of the inning. Harris registered three straight strikeouts to clinch the win, then ran to Milo, hoisting him high in the air.

Cody found Murphy huddled in a corner of one of the softball dugouts, as far away from the baseball dugouts as one could get and still be within the complex. His chin drooped to his chest and he was muttering something. At first Cody thought he was praying. But after hearing a bit of the language the third baseman was using, he knew this was no prayer.

"Hey, Murph," he said. "That was a tough play you tried to make. Those slow rollers are killers. You okay?"

Murphy didn't look up. "Yeah, I guess so. I'm so stupid. Coach is probably going to bench me next game. I'm sorry I lost us the game."

Cody sat next to his teammate. "You didn't lose it. I mean, look at me, going one-for-four. I'm not even hitting my weight so far this season."

Murphy smacked his hand on the bench. "At least you didn't make an error. You know, last season I didn't make a single error. And the year before that I had only two. Now this. My concentration is lousy lately. It's just—"

Cody cocked his head. "Just what?"

Murphy looked at him briefly and then turned away. "You lost your mom a while ago. To cancer, right?"

"Yeah."

"Well, my mom has it, too. It started as breast cancer but now it's everywhere. Her bones, her brain. Everywhere."

Cody exhaled slowly. *Please, God*, he prayed. *Help me help Murph. Help me be strong. Help me to focus on him, not my own sadness, which feels like it might swallow me again.*

He studied Murphy's sullen face for a few moments and then said slowly, "I know what you mean. It was the same thing with my mom. It's hard to play carrying that kind of weight around inside. It's hard to focus. You try to get away from it, but it just keeps creeping back on you."

"Tell me about it."

"Does Coach know about your situation?"

"No. I mean, what am I supposed to do? Have my dad write a note that says, 'Please excuse AJ if he occasionally plays like a stiff. His mom is dying'? Besides, I don't get the impression that Coach Lathrop would care. He's one cold dude."

"Well, maybe I can say something to him, if that's okay with you."

"I guess so. I do wish he knew that I wouldn't make an error like that, not under normal circumstances."

Cody stood to go. He felt a flood of words pressing to escape from his mouth. But which ones could he release, and which ones needed to be held back? He remembered all the well-intentioned but stinging clichés people peppered him with in the weeks after his mother's death— "At least she's not suffering any-more." "She's gone to a better place." "It was God's will, and you must not question his sovereign will, young man." "Cody, you must be grateful for the time you did have with her—some children grow up without a mother." Or his least favorite—"Your dad is young and quite handsome—he'll find a new wife soon. Just you wait and see!"

The only guy who always seemed to know the right words to say was Blake.

Blake. Cody smiled as the name flashed in his mind. "Hey, Murph," he began tentatively, "I don't want to go giving you advice, because you're probably getting a lot of that, but can I suggest something?"

"I guess so. I mean, you're probably the only person in the whole town who knows what this is like."

"Well, there's this guy, Blake Randall. He's cool, and he really helped me when my mom died. He's still helping me, in fact. He's the youth director at Crossroads Community, my church, and—"

"Church?"

Cody didn't like the way the word sounded, coming from Murphy's mouth. "Uh, yeah."

Murphy wagged his head slowly. "Look, I appreciate that you're trying to help, but I don't need God, man. I need my mom to be well again. I need my mom back."

Cody nodded. "I understand what you're saying. When I had to watch my mom die slowly, there were times I didn't want anything to do with God. Other times I was mad at him. But I found out that when it all went down, I needed him more than ever. So think about talking to Blake. He comes to all our games. He's the skinny guy with the Yankees baseball cap and the ugly gray shorts. Maybe I can at least introduce you to him?"

"I guess so. But I'm not joining any church or anything."

"Nobody's asking you to. I just want you to know that there are people who care. Blake's one of them. So am I."

"Thanks, Cody. Now, if you don't mind—"

Cody headed up the dugout steps. "You need some time alone. I understand."

The Rockies earned their first win of the season against a team from Maranatha Christian School's summer program. Brett Evans scattered five hits—all singles—over seven innings in a 7–1 victory. Pork Chop launched his third homer in as many games, and Cody smacked his first extra-base hit of the season, a line drive over the shortstop's head that led to a stand-up double.

Murphy committed his second error of the season, overrunning a dribbler down the third base line. Cody sprinted in from the outfield to console him when the inning ended. "Those slow rollers are a bear to field," he said, loudly enough for everyone to hear. "I think in the majors they would have scored that as a base hit."

After the win at Maranatha, the Rockies dropped a pair of road games, and Coach Lathrop quit talking about getting a win in postseason play. In fact, he quit talking about much of anything.

In the second road loss, the Rockies faced the Braves again. This time their pitcher was Rollins, a lefty with devastating stuff. He repeatedly handcuffed Pork Chop with a wicked backdoor slider and shut down the rest of the Rockies with a missile of a fastball. For good measure, he plunked Cody squarely in the ribs during his last at bat.

Great, Cody thought as he trotted gingerly to first base. *The only thing I'm going to lead the team in is bruises.*

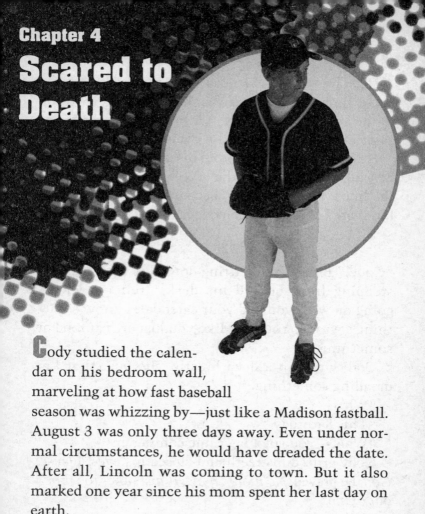

Chapter 4
Scared to Death

Cody studied the calendar on his bedroom wall, marveling at how fast baseball season was whizzing by—just like a Madison fastball. August 3 was only three days away. Even under normal circumstances, he would have dreaded the date. After all, Lincoln was coming to town. But it also marked one year since his mom spent her last day on earth.

"It's just a day," he muttered to himself. "Why be so afraid of it? I mean, why not worry about August second or fourth? What is it about the one-year mark that has me so freaked out?"

He stared at the calendar some more. He thought about finding a black marker and completely filling in the square for that day. "Yeah," he whispered sarcastically, "like that's really going to help."

He grabbed the phone from his nightstand. "Blake," he said when he heard the voice on the other end of the line, "I gotta see you, because I must be trippin'. I'm scared of my own calendar!"

"Code," Blake said, putting down his legal pad and stepping from behind his desk, "tell me what's going on with you and your calendar. I know something's wrong. You look like you just ate cat food or something."

Cody drew in a deep breath. "It's just that I'm dreading something."

"What?"

"This Saturday."

"What—you got a big game coming up?"

Cody gritted his teeth and closed his eyes. *Please, God,* he prayed. *No more crying. It just takes too much out of me.*

Blake was saying something. Cody had missed the first part of it, but now he heard, "I'm sorry, Cody. I just realized. About Saturday. It's August third. That's what's bothering you."

Cody stared at the ceiling. "Yeah. The one-year anniversary of Mom's death. I've been dreading it for, like, months. 'Cuz I know it's all going to come back—all the emotions. Especially the sadness I felt when she died. The kind that seems like it'll totally crush me sometimes. And I know I'll remember how awkward and painful it was to be around the team, even the people at church."

Blake smiled sadly. "They treated you differently."

"Some of them did. It was like I had leprosy or something. Then, with the guys on the team—they didn't know what to say. I remember Alston and Gage joking around in the van on the way back from this tournament in the Springs. And I'm thinking, *How can you be laughing and joking around, you idiots? My mom's dead! Dead!* I wasn't just mad at them. I was mad at the sun for shining and the birds for singing. I wanted to smack anybody who was smiling."

Blake nodded. "When my dad died of the heart attack, I wanted to puke every time some bubbly pop song came on the radio. And for the first time in my life, I noticed how fake those laugh tracks on old TV reruns sound. The truth is, I was mad at life simply for going on. I just wanted everything to stop—at least for a while. What I needed was a National Month of Mourning."

Cody plopped down in a metal folding chair and looked up at Blake. "You know, you're, like, the only one who seems to understand the way I feel."

Blake shrugged. "I try."

"So, it's been two years since your dad died."

"Yes."

"Why are you smiling, B?"

"Because you said the word *died*. You know, it seems like lots of people are afraid of that word. They say 'passed away,' 'went to his reward,' or 'found his rest.' As if softening the words will soften the pain, alter the reality of what happened."

"Yeah. But in the end, you die."

"True. But then you live again."

"My mom was so sure of that. I have my doubts sometimes. But she knew. She told me that. And she was always honest. When I start to question heaven and everything, I remind myself that my mom would never lie about something that important."

Blake nodded solemnly.

Cody stood and backed toward the door. "So, I have practice in a few. Before I go, are you going to tell me how I'm going to get through this Saturday, or not?"

"I don't know, Cody. But I believe God will show you a way. Just as he did for me."

"How did you do it?"

Blake pointed to the doorway. "That's a story for another day. Go to practice. You don't get to practice much once the season starts, so take advantage of the time. By the way, sorry I couldn't make your last game. How's the rib? I heard you got beaned last week."

Cody shrugged. "It only hurts when I cough. Or laugh."

Blake nodded.

"Or breathe."

Blake smiled paternally. "Just stop doing those things and you should be fine."

"Thanks for your compassion, B."

"Hey, seriously, I can tape those ribs for you if you want. Remember, I was a trainer for my high school basketball team one year."

"Aw, I don't know, man—"

Blake popped to his feet. "Sit down, dude. We have some tape and stuff in the first aid kit. Prepare to be mummified."

Even with Blake's "mummy special," practice brought agony for Cody. He winced every time he threw the ball, and the first time he swung during batting practice, the pain almost robbed him of his breath. It felt like someone was driving a railroad spike into his side.

Coach Lathrop probably would have yelled at him, but he seemed more intent on reading an auto racing magazine while he sat sullenly in the dugout.

Pork Chop approached Cody after practice and gently laid a hand on his shoulder. "Dawg, are you sure you shouldn't get those ribs X-rayed or something?"

Cody carefully drew in a breath. "Nah, it's okay. They're getting better. Yesterday the pain was devastating. Today it's only excruciating. Besides, I think Dad's too busy to take me to the doctor. If he's not working crazy hours, he and Beth are off doing something. Dates or whatever." Cody sighed heavily. "*Date.* I hate that word."

Pork Chop nodded understandingly. "I know that's gotta be weird to you, my brother. But I bet it's helping your dad deal with his pain. Love's good for pain, man."

The words rang in Cody's ears.

"Code—dawg," he heard Pork Chop saying now. "Are you okay?"

Cody blinked. "Huh?"

"Where did you just go in your mind, man? You got this far-off look in your eyes."

"I guess I was just thinking—wondering."

"About what?"

"Lots of things. Like why Murph wasn't at practice today. I'm worried. His mom is sick. Really sick."

Cody checked phone messages as soon as he got home. The fourth one was from AJ Murphy. His voice was weak and hoarse. "Cody, I just felt like I should call you. She's gone. My mom's gone. Would you mind telling Coach? My dad, he's not doing well. I don't want to ask him to do anything right now. Anyway, thanks for everything. I gotta go now. Bye."

Cody burned up the phone lines for the next two hours. Blake was the first call. He promised he would reach out to the Murphy family and work with the people at the funeral home to make arrangements for the service.

Then he tried to call AJ, but no one was answering at the Murphy home. The next day, with the Lincoln game and the Dreaded Anniversary only two days away, Cody learned that the service would be held Sunday afternoon, the day after the game.

That night as he lay in bed, praying for comfort for the Murphys, an idea formed in Cody's mind. If it hadn't been 11 p.m., he would have put the plan into action right then. But he knew it would have to wait eight hours.

Cody was stretching out after a five-mile afternoon run with Drew when the doorbell rang. After checking to make sure it wasn't a guy in a suit peddling some kind of religion, he opened the door.

"Oh, hi, Beth."

She smiled at him. She smiled too wide. "Hey, Code! Is Luke back from work yet?"

Cody cleared his throat. "My dad isn't back yet."

Beth shrugged. "Uh, can I come in?"

Cody stepped back from the door. "Sure. I'm kind of busy, so . . . uh—"

"It's okay," Beth said, stepping across the threshold. "You don't have to entertain me. I think SportsCenter is on. But what are you so busy with? I thought you'd be watching ESPN."

Cody looked around, as if seeking a place to run and hide.

"Well—"

Beth giggled. "Well, what? What are you up to that you don't want to tell me about—something illegal?"

Cody tried to laugh. All that came out was a cough. "No, see, this guy on our baseball team, AJ Murphy—"

"Third baseman. Decent glove. Great arm. I know him from the games I've seen. Is he okay?"

"Not really. See, his mom died yesterday. Cancer, you know."

It looked to Cody that Beth might try to hug him. He crossed his arms across his chest so she'd know not to try.

"I'm sorry to hear it," she said quietly. "So, what are you busy with—it has something to do with AJ?"

"Yeah."

"Anything I can help with?"

"Not really. Thanks, though, but I got this one covered."

"Okay, but you let me know if you think of something I can do."

Cody shrugged. "Well, I might need a ride to the funeral Sunday afternoon."

"Done. You just tell me when you need to be there."

Cody headed for the stairs, then glanced back. "If you and Dad end up having something planned, don't worry about it. I'm sure I can find a ride somehow."

Beth shook her head. "We have no plans. And if we did, we'd break 'em. This is important to you. So it's important to your dad. And to me, too. And it's not just important to me because of your dad—it's important to me because of you."

Cody nodded and bounded up the stairs, three at a time, nearly crying out in pain with each step. He spent another hour on the phone. After making his last call of the day, he hung up. "It's coming together," he whispered hopefully. "Please, God, let this plan be what I think it can be."

Saturday, the one-year anniversary of Linda Martin's death, brought the Lincoln Lancers to town. "The bad news," Coach Lathrop told the Rockies before the game, "is that we have to play Lincoln today. The good news is that Madison isn't pitching. I guess he's gone the distance in his last two games, and they're resting his arm for the postseason. He's gonna play shortstop. So Lincoln will send Locke to the hill instead of Madman."

"Locke's no slouch," Pork Chop whispered to Cody. "I hope he doesn't remember how you hung that bagel on him during basketball, or he might throw you some chin music."

Cody rolled his eyes. "Thanks, Chop. I was just feeling good that I wouldn't have Madman head hunting me today, and now you go and ruin it."

Locke was no Madison, but he mixed his pitches well, keeping the Rockies off balance with a fastball, slider, curve, and changeup. No one got a hit off him for the first three innings.

For the home team, Bart Evans started off erratically—surrendering two runs in both the first and second innings. But he settled down in the third, sitting the Lancers down in order. Then, after giving up a leadoff walk to open the fourth, he struck out Locke and Madison. He wrapped up the inning by catching the runner at first taking too big a lead. He picked him off, and the Rockies headed to their half of the inning only four runs behind.

Grant quickly closed the gap to one. Gage Mc-Clintock hit a bloop single, advanced to second on Locke's errant pickoff attempt, stole third, and scored on a sacrifice fly off the bat of Mark Goddard. Locke walked the next batter he faced, and then Alston hit his first homer of the season, a rainbow shot to left.

Bart kept the Lancer batters in check the rest of the way, and the Rockies headed to the bottom of the seventh still trailing only 4–3.

Cody led off the inning, resolving to keep his swing compact to protect his aching ribs. Locke's first pitch was in on his hands, but he chopped at it anyway, hitting a bouncer to third. As he chugged to first base, he saw the ball take a bad hop and leap above the third baseman's glove—into his Adam's apple.

Alston swung on the first pitch he saw, swatting a hard grounder that looked like it might escape the infield. However, Nelson, the Lincoln first baseman, chased it down, and Locke did a great job of hustling over to cover first. Alston was out by a step, but Cody advanced to second on the play.

Come on, Brett, he pleaded silently as he caught his breath. *Just get a base knock and I'll tie this game for us. A double would be nice. With these ribs, I'm not sure I can score on a single.*

Locke's first two pitches were down in the strike zone, and Brett, not a good low-ball hitter, watched them both without so much as twitching his bat.

"Come on, Brett," Cody heard Pork Chop holler from the on deck circle, "you gotta go down and get those!"

Locke's third pitch was low and hard, and Brett, looking more like Tiger Woods than a baseball player, golfed it toward third.

Cody bolted from second the instant he saw Brett make contact. As he labored toward third, he saw Madison standing directly in his way, posed like a statue. Gardener, the Lancer third baseman, was charging forward to snare the ball, but Madison wasn't moving over to cover the bag for him.

Cody knew a collision was inevitable. He veered slightly to his right, trying to avoid hitting the other player without leaving the base path. He felt his hip strike Madison's. Madison hit the ground. Cody was knocked off balance for a moment, but he quickly found his stride and dashed to third.

Madison bounced up as if he were made of rubber, and marched toward third. "What was that?" he screamed, his head so close to Cody's that the brims of their caps almost touched.

Cody shrugged. "I was running a straight line from second to third, and you were planted right in my path. You interfered."

"What?!"

Cody glanced over his shoulder and saw Gage's dad, who was coaching third, striding toward them. Then he returned his focus to his opponent. "You heard me, Madison," he said, fighting to keep his voice from shaking—or shooting up two octaves. "You can't interfere with the runner. I'm sure you didn't mean to. After all, you're more used to pitching than playing short. But still—"

Madison's mouth fell open so wide that Cody could see his tonsils. "You must be crazy, homey. If we play you guys again and I'm pitching, you best watch your head!"

Mr. McClintock was between them now. "Settle down, son," he said to Madison. "It's just a game."

Madison glowered at Mr. McClintock but said nothing.

Meanwhile, the Lincoln coach was at home plate, arguing with the umpire. Eventually he thrust both arms into the air, as if directing a choir, then stomped away. Brett had been called out at first, but Cody was officially awarded third base. Pork Chop came up to bat, smiled in Cody's direction, and then laced the first pitch he saw deep into the gap in left field. Cody knew he could trot in safely, but he sprinted all the way home anyway, making sure to touch the plate.

He turned to see Pork Chop pull into second with a stand-up double. As Cody headed to the dugout, he could tell Chop was saying something to Madison, no doubt inviting him, "Hey, Madman—why don't you stand in *my* way this time? They'll have to bring in a team of archeologists to find your remains in the dirt when I'm done with you!"

Goddard struck out, and Lincoln went on to win in extra innings, but the Lancers seemed more angry than elated when the game ended. And as the two teams lined up single file for the traditional postgame handshakes, Madison was conspicuously absent.

Cody didn't have time to agonize about the loss. Sunday was only a day away—it was time to see if his plan would succeed.

That night, just before he fell asleep, Cody whispered a quiet prayer. "God, I feel kinda weird. With the game today, and my being so nervous about the funeral tomorrow, I sort of survived the day without being too sad about Mom. But now I feel bad. I don't want her to think that the day wasn't significant. I want her to know that I'm still sad she's gone. So, if it's okay to ask, please can you let her know that I miss her? And that what I've been working on these past couple of days is one way of honoring her? Thank you and amen."

Cody paced nervously in the parking lot of Crossroads Community Church. He looked at his watch. It read 1:57. The service was going to start in three minutes. "Come on, guys," he whispered, "where are you?"

He was about ready to give up and go inside when Doug's Camry screeched around the corner, followed by Mr. McClintock's minivan.

"You had me worried," Cody said to Pork Chop as he spilled from the backseat. "What took you so long?"

Pork Chop looked at Doug, who slammed the driver's-side door shut, then shot his little brother an accusing stare.

"It's my fault," Chop muttered. "I had a pants problem."

Cody shrugged his shoulders. "A pants problem? What—did you get a hole in 'em or something?"

"Nah, man, it's just that the last time I wore these pants, well, that was about ten pounds ago. I had to lie down on the bed to get these on—and, dawg, if I so much as sneeze, the little button at the top of these pants is gonna pop off so hard that it might hurt somebody."

Cody wagged his head and heard himself laughing. "Well then, don't sneeze." He studied Chop's navy blue suit. The cuffs of the pants hung at his ankle bones, revealing about an inch and a half of what Cody was sure were white athletic socks. *Well*, he thought, *at least he's wearing socks. That's better than nothing.*

"You look sharp, Chop."

"Thanks, dawg. You clean up nice yourself. I like that blazer. I haven't seen you wear that since—" Pork Chop stopped himself in midsentence. "Ah, man, I'm sorry."

Cody took a deep breath. "It's okay. Besides, Mom's funeral wasn't the last time I wore it. I wore it Easter Sunday. You would've known that if you had come with me. Now, let's get the rest of the team together and get inside."

Someone had roped off the third row of pews on the left side of the auditorium. A somber usher directed the twelve well-dressed teens to their place. Robyn was sitting in the fourth row. She gave Cody an understanding smile and nodded at him as he passed by.

A rail-thin man with wispy blond hair was playing "Surely Goodness and Mercy" on the organ as the Rockies filed into the pews. AJ and his father sat in a front-row pew, on the right-hand side of the church. Cody saw Murph's dad turn around and then tap his son on the shoulder. Murph turned as well, and Cody's eyes met his.

Cody didn't speak, didn't nod, didn't smile. He just held AJ Murphy's gaze for a few seconds. And when his new friend turned back toward the front of the church, Cody knew they had shared an hour conversation's worth of thoughts and emotions.

Pastor Taylor stepped to the podium and began reading from Psalm 23. When he came to the end— "and I shall dwell in the house of the Lord forever"— Cody heard himself whisper, "Amen."

Pork Chop, who was sitting next to Cody, made a fist and held it out to him. Cody made a fist of his own and exchanged daps with his best friend.

Pastor Taylor was addressing the congregation now. He said, "We have welcomed the Murphys into our community. And now we need to make sure the welcome doesn't end. We must surround them with God's love."

Cody watched AJ as the service continued. And he felt again what it was like to endure the funeral of the person who gave you life. Mr. Murphy tried to comfort AJ occasionally, draping his arm around his son and squeezing his shoulder. But then he would withdraw his arm and bury his face in his hands, sobbing quietly.

Just before the service ended, Cody saw AJ play the role of comforter, putting his arm around his dad. The sight of it was like a kick to the heart. Cody swallowed hard.

Dear heavenly Father, he prayed earnestly, *only you know how bad AJ is hurting right now—although I think I have a pretty good idea. Please comfort him. I hope the team being here will help somehow. I hope we can all show him he's not alone. Please show us— show me—what to do.*

After the service ended, the Rockies found AJ in the church foyer. They surrounded him and, one by one, offered their condolences.

"I'm sorry," Cody heard Alston say, his voice halting. "I can't imagine what it must be like. I don't know if it will help, but just know that I'll have your back when high school starts. I've got lots of friends up there. We'll look out for you."

Pork Chop was next. He wrapped a thick right arm around AJ's shoulder. "Ditto what Alston said, man. My condolences to you and your family."

When it was Cody's turn, he stood in front of Murph, waiting for the right words to come to him.

They came to A. J. instead. "It hurts, Cody."

Cody took a deep breath. "I know."

"But it would hurt a lot worse if you and the team weren't here. Thanks. I'll never forget this."

Later, after Cody and his fellow mourners had politely picked at an assortment of finger foods and desserts in the church fellowship hall, he stood with Blake and Pork Chop in the parking lot.

"You okay, dawg?" Chop asked.

Cody thought for a minute. "Yeah, I think I am. It's weird. I mean, don't get me wrong. I would give anything to have my mom back. But because of what happened to me, I was able to help Murph. Help him in a way I probably couldn't have otherwise."

Blake smiled thoughtfully. "Even in the most tragic circumstances, we know that God is still working for our good."

"I don't get it," Chop said, squirming and sweating in his too-tight suit. "You're not saying Cody's mom was supposed to die so he'd know how to help Murph, are you? 'Cuz that would be whack!"

"No, I'm not saying that at all. I'm just saying that God is working for our good even when the worst stuff happens."

Chop shook his head. "Man, that's weird."

Blake smiled again. "Not weird, my friend. Mysterious. God can work in mysterious ways. Miraculous ways. Right, Cody?"

Before Cody could answer, A. J.'s father approached him. "Young man," he said, leveling tired gray eyes at him, "thank you for what you and the team did today. You are a godsend."

Mr. Murphy paused, appearing to search for more words. Then he turned and walked stiffly to the middle of the parking lot, where he stopped and craned his neck to the sky, as if looking for answers.

Cody could see he was beginning to cry. "It's okay, Phil," he heard someone call out to him.

Cody shuddered in spite of himself. He thought of the year that had passed. *No, Phil,* he thought. *It'll be a long time before things are okay. But I'm gonna do all I can to make them that way for your son. And maybe somehow that will help you, too.*

Chapter 5
Taking One for the Team

The Rockies sputtered to an anemic 2–8 regular-season record, which earned them the bottom seed in the postseason tournament—and therefore the dubious privilege of facing Lincoln in the first round.

Two days before the tournament in Colorado Springs, A. J. called Cody and told him he wouldn't be able to play.

"I feel bad that I'm letting the team down," he said. "But I think I would let you guys down even worse if I tried to play, you know?"

"Don't worry, Murph," Cody assured him. "The guys will understand. And if by some miracle we beat Lincoln, I'm bringing you the game ball."

"Well, I won't hold my breath for that," Murph said, mustering a brave laugh.

"This is a nice field," Pork Chop observed moments before the first game of the tournament. "Big, too. Two-eighty-five to straightaway center. I'd love to send one out there."

Cody looked in the direction Chop was pointing. The gently sloping hill behind the outfield's chain-link fence looked like the world's most bizarre checkerboard. An assortment of square picnic blankets—grays, greens, blues, yellows, and one with purple polka dots—were scattered across the grass.

Families sat, enjoying pregame picnics, while dogs and young children romped around. Cody smiled as he saw one toddler chasing another, wielding a plastic bat over his head like a club.

A few older spectators sat in lawn chairs with cup holders, no doubt sipping sodas and lemonade.

Cody glanced up at the nearly cloudless sky. "It's a perfect day for baseball. Too bad we're gonna get spanked."

"Maybe not," said Brett Evans, who was swinging his right arm nearby. "Maybe not."

Pork Chop raised his eyebrows at Cody. "Dawg, Brett's got his game face on."

"Yeah," Cody answered. "But so will Madman."

Cody stepped to the plate to open the game. He felt Madison's focus on him, like the pinpoint beam of sunlight through a magnifying glass, and shuddered. The glare seemed hot enough to burn a hole in his face.

He tightened his grip on the bat. He thought he saw Madison smirk as he rocked back and brought both hands up to his face.

Here it comes, Cody told himself. *Focus!*

Madison grunted as he released the ball. Cody forced his eyes wide open. The ball was speeding toward him, fast and high. He fought the urge to bail out—to lurch from the batter's box or dive to the ground. He saw—even felt—the ball go speeding past his eyes, a buzzing white blur that seemed electrically charged.

Owens, Lincoln's catcher, had to leap from his crouch to snare it. Cody heard him groan when the ball exploded into his mitt like a firecracker.

"Ball!" the umpire bellowed.

Cody stepped out of the batter's box and tightened the Velcro strap on his batting glove as Owens tossed the ball back to Madison. "Man," the catcher said as he settled back into his crouch, "Madman's throwing fire today. I wouldn't want to be you, Martin."

Cody said nothing but felt his head nodding in agreement. *I'm not sure I want to be me, either.*

Madison's second pitch kicked up dirt two feet in front of home plate. Why he swung at it, Cody wasn't sure. He heard Owens laughing as he dug the ball out of the dirt and handed it to the ump for inspection.

The umpire turned the ball over and over in his giant right hand, as if he were examining an apple at the grocery store. Finally he deemed the ball playable and lobbed it to Madison.

The third pitch was perfect—a bullet right down the middle of the plate. Cody thought the ball might have already smacked into Owens' glove before he swung.

Madison's next offering was a changeup. Cody was completely fooled by Madison's whiplike arm motion. He swung before the ball was anywhere near home plate. "Strike three!" the umpire roared.

The Lancers' pitcher shook his head and gave Cody a subtle bye-bye wave as he headed for the dugout.

Madison struck out the next two batters as well. Cody found himself feeling guilty that he was relieved when it happened. *Some team player I am*, he scolded himself. *I'm more worried about looking bad than I am about my teammates' performance.*

As the Rockies jogged to take their positions in the field, Cody saw concern, not the usual confidence, in

Pork Chop's eyes. "We're in trouble," he said, shaking his head.

Brett Evans always kept his cap pulled down low on his forehead, so it was hard to tell what was in his eyes. But from the way he was pitching, it must have been fire.

Brett had no part of Madison's arm strength, but he was smart—and a master at locating pitches. Through the first three innings, he moved the ball around the strike zone so well that no Lincoln hitter could solve him.

Cody smiled, thinking, *It's as if Brett's playing pin the tail on the donkey—without a blindfold.*

In the fourth, Locke connected with a hanging curveball, but he got too far under it, and Alston gathered it in just a step in front of the warning track. Owens followed, lacing a hard liner toward Bart Evans, who had taken Murphy's position at third. Bart went deep into the hole, backhanded the ball on one hop, and gunned a perfect throw to Chop at first.

After Owens was called out, Brett pointed at his brother, showing his gratitude.

"This is quite a pitcher's duel," Coach Lathrop observed before the start of the fifth. He looked at

Brett. "Both you and Mr. Madison have no-hitters going. You just stay focused, you hear? We can beat these guys."

Cody was the second man up in the fifth, and Madison struck him out on three pitches, one of which Cody was certain he didn't even see. Chop gave Madison a scare later in the inning when he smacked a two-out changeup deep into right field. However, it hooked foul at the last possible moment.

Madison pounded his mitt against his hip, muttering to himself. He looked to his dugout and then threw two pitches in the dirt. Pork Chop drew a walk, glaring at Madison as he jogged to first. Madison sneered back at him and then struck out Brett Evans on four pitches.

Madison blanked the Rockies again in the sixth, then got his team off to a promising start in the Lincoln half of the inning. He fouled off four pitches before drawing a walk. He took second on a passed ball that Goddard couldn't dig out of the dirt.

Angry with himself for the bad pitch, Brett bore down and struck out the batter, as well as the next one he faced. However, Madison stole third in the process.

Lincoln sent out a left-handed pinch hitter to try to bring in the game's first run. Brett missed badly on his first two pitches but then found the zone. Madison hopped up and down in anger when the umpire called a waist-high fastball, "Strike three!"

"Last inning, men," Pork Chop said in the dugout. "We can do this! Come on! Let's get Brett a no-hitter, and us a big W!"

Cody saw Bart Evans whispering something to his brother, a hand on his shoulder. Brett nodded solemnly.

Gage McClintock led off the inning. After taking a called first strike, he laid down a decent bunt that trickled up the first base line. Madison charged after the ball, snared it, and whirled to throw to first. Gage was running hard, but Cody, who was on deck, shook his head dejectedly.

Gage has no shot, he thought.

Cody thought wrong. In his zeal to throw out the runner, Madison sailed the ball two feet over the outstretched mitt of Nelson, the first baseman.

Before he headed to the plate, Cody felt himself being tugged backward. Coach Lathrop's eyes were burning with intensity—or was it desperation?

"Listen to me, Martin," he said, thin lips pulled tightly across clenched yellowing teeth. "I want this win. So we're gonna manufacture a run. Madison's been throwing inside at you all day. So I want you to lean into the strike zone and get yourself on base, you understand?"

Cody looked up at his coach. "But, sir," he said, "my ribs are really hurting. They might even be broken. I, uh—"

"I don't care if your ribs are broken. I don't care if your stinkin' heart is broken. You do what I say. Listen to me—you do *not* want to disobey me on this. Understand?"

Cody nodded. "Yes sir," he said quietly.

Madison's first two pitches were over the outside part of the plate—one a called strike, the other a ball. Cody swallowed hard. *Man, I never thought I'd be upset that Madman didn't throw inside on me. I mean, Coach Lathrop can't blame me for not leaning into those pitches, can he?*

Madison was smirking as he went into his windup for the third pitch. *You are so cocky, dude,* Cody thought. *I wish I could send a line drive right back at your face—and if I weren't almost petrified with fear, maybe I would.*

The third pitch was more high heat. Cody dove to the ground, hoping he could get his head down before he got plunked.

As Cody got up and brushed the dirt off his uniform, he saw Madison standing on the mound, smiling smugly, arms crossed, as if he were posing for a *Sports Illustrated* cover. Owens, meanwhile, had dashed to the backstop to retrieve the pitch, which he was unable to snag. Gage McClintock moved from first to second. Now Grant had a man in scoring position, with no outs.

"The count is two balls, one strike, on the batter, Cody Martin," he heard the public-address announcer say.

As he settled into his stance, Cody looked at Coach Lathrop, who was glowering at him from the dugout. Cody could read his coach's expression like writing on the wall—"You better let Madison hit you, or I'll hit you myself!"

Cody swallowed hard. *God,* he prayed silently, *I'm way over my head here. I don't know what to do. I've never disobeyed a coach's orders in my life, but—*

Cody's prayer was interrupted by the next pitch, a scorching fastball right down the middle of the plate.

"Steee-rike!" the umpire called.

Cody shook his head in disgust. *That's Madman's first decent pitch of this at bat, and yet I'm still one strike away from being out.*

As he dug his cleats into the dirt, anchoring himself for the next pitch, Cody sensed that Madison would throw inside this time. He shot a glance at Coach Lathrop. His hands were on his hips, and he looked like he might march to home plate any minute and grind his stubborn center fielder into the dirt.

Cody wanted to pray again, but Madison was already well into his windup. With a gorilla grunt, Madison fired his next pitch. Cody saw the ball bearing down on him like a heat-seeking missile. Fighting his instincts to run away and sign up for summer tennis, he leaned forward, dipping his shoulder toward home plate.

The ball hit him below his left armpit, the blow spinning him halfway around. The site of the impact felt as if it had caught fire.

Man, Cody thought as he closed his eyes and clenched his teeth, fighting back tears, *how can a* round *ball give such a* sharp *pain?* He felt his knees turning to gelatin, but he vowed not to go down. *I'm not gonna give you the satisfaction, Madman. No way.*

"Son," the umpire was saying to him, "you may take your base, but are you okay? Want me to call your coach out here?"

Cody looked to the dugout. *Coach Lathrop's gotta know I'm hurting*, he reasoned. *Maybe he'll send in a pinch runner. After all, he must have a heart somewhere in that barrel chest of his.*

But all the coach did was glare at him—hairy arms crossed defiantly across his torso.

Cody inhaled carefully. His ribs felt like they would crack if he took in too much air. He prepared to speak, hoping his words wouldn't come out as pathetic gasps.

"I'm fine, sir. Don't need a coach, don't need a trainer."

"Okay," the ump said, shaking his head. "Take your base, then. Batter up!"

Cody trotted to first. He could feel Madison's eyes on him, so he fought the urge to wince with every stride.

Nelson greeted him when he arrived. "You okay, dude? That one looked like it left a mark. Man, Madison's been throwing fire all year. But I think he's getting stronger every game."

Cody grimaced. "Just my luck."

Alston stood at the plate, taking a few vicious practice cuts. *He looks focused*, Cody noted. *If anybody can get a hit off Madman, it's gotta be TA.*

Three pitches later Cody shook his head sadly. *Or maybe not*, he thought. *I gotta give Madman credit. I can't even remember the last time I saw Alston whiff on three straight pitches!*

As Pork Chop settled into his stance, Cody saw Coach Lathrop signaling something to Gage, who nodded almost imperceptibly. Madison's first pitch was a low curveball, and Gage was off and running, right on cue.

He never had a chance. Owens popped up from his crouch and rocketed a perfect throw to third. Cody seized the opportunity and stole second, but the Lancers had erased the lead runner and accomplished out number two. At best, they'd view Cody's steal as minor collateral damage—if Madman could get Pork Chop out.

Madison tried too hard on his next pitch, rocketing it into the dirt to Owens' left. Owens managed to trap the ball under his chubby catcher's mitt, but Cody easily took third base on the play.

As Cody stood on third, catching his breath, he saw Pork Chop step out of the batter's box and look toward their coach. He couldn't believe the signal Coach Lathrop had offered.

Cody felt a sense of dread descend on him like a fog. *I can't believe he's callin' for a suicide squeeze,* he thought. *Chop isn't that good a bunter. He's too impatient. And besides, he likes to swing away. On the other hand, if I manage to steal home, we can beat these guys, and Brett will have a no-hitter. But if something goes wrong, I know I'm gonna get blamed, somehow. And here I thought I escaped my chance to be the goat. Man, who was I kidding! Madison hasn't lost a game all year. What made me think today would be any different!*

Cody watched the Lincoln pitcher with grudging admiration. He was giving Chop his best sneer as he went into his stretch.

Cody laughed to himself. *If you think you can intimidate Chop with that prune face, dude, you really are mad.*

Chop squared his body on the next pitch, but somehow he missed the ball. "Stee-rike!" the umpire bellowed.

Cody resisted the urge to kick third base in disgust. Now Madison was on to the Rockies' strategy. He was sure to avoid giving Chop a pitch he could bunt.

As Cody predicted, pitch number four was a chest-high screamer that Chop backed away from as if it had fangs. The umpire called the pitch a strike, bringing groans of disbelief from the Rockies fans.

The groans turned to cheers on the next pitch, which Madison seemed to locate in the exact spot as the previous effort. Only this time the call from behind the plate was, "Ball!"

With the count at three and two, Owens called time-out and jogged to the mound to discuss strategy with his pitcher.

While the two Lancers powwowed, Chop turned to Cody, cocking his head slightly.

Cody nodded in return. *I know exactly what you're wondering, dude. Madison has to get this pitch in the strike zone, or he puts the fastest big man in the free world on base. So you just get a bunt in play, and yeah, I'll sprint home for all I'm worth, ribs or no ribs.*

Cody studied Madison's face and saw something he'd never seen there before—concern.

Madison growled as he fired a low, hard fastball. It might have been called a ball, but Chop took no chances. He squared his body and executed a textbook bunt that crawled through the grass toward the pitcher's mound. Cody, his heart jackhammering, dashed for home. Each stride brought a crushing pain down his side, but he didn't care. *I'll cry tomorrow,* he thought as he ran.

Owens was a good catcher. He tore off his mask and hustled for the ball. He secured it before it got halfway to the mound, then pivoted and raced Cody to home plate.

Cody tried not to think about how much more pain he was about to invite into his left side and dove head-first, stretching his arms toward the plate. He heard himself cry out as he slid under Owens' attempted tag. He looked up to see the umpire signal him safe before he closed his eyes, trying to shut out the agony. Amid all the din coming from the stands and the dugouts and the field, Pork Chop's voice rang the loudest. "That's my dawg!" he was shouting. "That is *my* dawg!"

As if assisting a person made of eggshells, Mr. McClintock helped Cody to his feet. "You okay?"

"My ribs," Cody gasped. "Not good."

As Cody lowered himself carefully onto the dugout bench, he felt Coach Lathrop hovering above him. He was smiling, for the first time in weeks. "That's the way to do it, Martin," he said, too loudly. "That's the way to play ball for me."

Cody looked up and offered a weak smile. *I didn't do it for you*, he thought. *I did it for Brett. For Murph. For my mom. Maybe even for me. But that wasn't about you.*

Meanwhile, Pork Chop had made it to first on the squeeze play, but he would go no farther. Madison struck out the next Rocky, and Cody found himself shaking his head in admiration. "The guy doesn't lose his focus," he whispered. "You gotta give him credit for that."

As the Rockies prepared to take the field, Coach Lathrop was screaming, "No letdowns! No mistakes! Don't you dare let this one get away. I want this so bad, I can taste it!"

Amid the rant, Cody saw Chop approach Brett and put his arm around him. "Just keep throwing strikes, my brother. We got your back. We are gonna be a wall behind you."

Coach Lathrop took Cody out of the game, shifting Alston to center and putting Terrance Dylan, who recently joined the team after recovering from a broken ankle, in right. "I don't want you to risk injuring yourself," the coach said to Cody. "We need to protect you, understand?"

Cody nodded. *Yeah, now that you got what you wanted outta me, you're all of a sudden concerned. Whatever.*

He stood and moved to the front of the dugout to watch Brett battle for his first no-hitter. He knew he would have to talk to Blake about the proper attitude a fourteen-year-old is supposed to take when an adult is lying to him.

I don't want to have a disrespectful attitude, he prayed as he watched Brett strike out batter number one, *but I don't respect liars, Lord, and I know you don't, either. Does Coach really think I believe he cares about protecting me? I mean, how short does he think my memory is?*

Nelson was up now, and Brett quickly got ahead of him, one ball and two strikes. Nelson popped up the next pitch in foul territory near third. Bart Evans waved everyone away frantically, screaming, "Mine! All mine!"

He secured the ball in his mitt, squeezing it so tightly that Cody thought it might disintegrate. Then Bart nodded at his brother and held up his forefinger and pinkie, signaling that the Rockies were one out away from the shutout.

Locke represented Lincoln's last chance. He wasn't a power hitter, but he almost always made contact. Cody stared into the outfield. Alston was playing him a bit shallow.

I think I'd play him a little deeper than that, he reasoned. *But then again, I don't have wheels like Alston.*

Locke smacked Brett's first offering toward left. Cody felt his fists clench. *If that's a fair ball, it's extra bases,* he thought to himself.

Cody saw Coach Lathrop spin 180 degrees and sit for a moment on the ground in front of the dugout when the third base umpire called the ball foul.

"Oh, man," the coach moaned. "That was close. Too close. Brett's getting tired."

Cody wondered if he might consider a relief pitcher. He could move Bart over to pitcher without risking a mutiny from the Evans family. Maybe. But then he saw Brett throw his hardest fastball of the game. Locke couldn't do anything but admire it as it whizzed by.

Cody chuckled to himself. *Who am I kidding? I bet we couldn't push Brett off that mound with a bulldozer.*

On the next pitch, Brett tried to get Locke to bite on a fastball out of the strike zone, but he kept his bat still, shaking his head at Brett as the umpire called, "Ball!"

Now would be a good time for your curve, Cody urged silently. *You haven't thrown a hook since early in the game. Come on, Brett, cross him up. He'll be sitting on your fastball.*

Ten seconds later Cody's intuition was proven correct.

Brett groaned as he brought the gas one more time. The pitch was belt-high as it crossed the outside of the plate, and Locke gave it a ride deep to center field.

For a moment silence engulfed the field. Then, as if someone had flicked on the world's biggest TV, the place was buzzing with screams and shouts of expectation—or dread.

Alston half-turned and tracked the ball as it sailed toward the fence in straightaway center. Cody saw him stay focused on the ball's arc, even as his feet hit the warning track. Then, as the ball headed down, Alston leaped so high that Cody thought he might rocket right out of his cleats.

"Man," he heard himself say, "Alston's going to be dunking in basketball next year, for sure!"

But for today, Alston was merely jumping at just the right angle to lean his body over the fence and snag Locke's fly ball in the end of his webbing, robbing the Lancers of a sure home run.

Cody thought Alston might spike the ball or toss it into the air in celebration. After all, he was the biggest showboater in the state of Colorado. But instead he grabbed the ball from his mitt and, holding it out in front of him, sprinted directly toward Brett, who was embracing his brother on the pitcher's mound, the two of them bouncing up and down as if they were on pogo sticks.

Alston got to the mound and offered the ball to Brett, patting the pitcher on the back, and Brett took the memento in both hands.

"Terry Alston," Cody said to no one in particular, "there's hope for you yet."

Cody joined the postgame celebration on the pitcher's mound, cringing every time a teammate clapped him on the back. *It's worth it*, he kept telling himself. *It's so worth it.*

After the jubilee he headed for the stands. His dad and Beth had shown up late in the second inning, but at least they made it. He couldn't see them now, but he did spot Pork Chop's two most significant others.

"Where's my dad?" Cody asked Mr. Porter and Doug as he carefully made his way up the aluminum bleachers toward them.

Chop's father chuckled and nudged his elder son, who started chuckling, too. "Last time I saw him," Mr. Porter said, "he and Beth were behind the backstop, reading your coach the riot act."

Cody tilted his head and frowned. "You gotta be kiddin'."

"It's true," Doug affirmed. "They were gettin' medieval on ol' Coach Lathrop."

"But . . . I don't get it—"

"You might not be getting it," Mr. Porter said, "but your coach sure is!"

Cody ran down the bleachers, taking them two rows at a time and "oofing" in pain with each step.

His dad and Beth flanked Coach Lathrop. Luke Martin had his arms folded over his chest, which Cody was sure he was puffing out to make it bigger than it really was. Beth was brandishing her index finger like a sword, right under the coach's nose.

"Don't you dare try to deny it, sir," she was scolding him. "We have the word of several of Cody's teammates. You were aware of his injury and you told him to lean into a fastball from maybe the hardest-throwing pitcher in the state. That is just wrong!"

"Look," Coach Lathrop fired back, "don't you tell me how to do my job. Who are you, anyway? You're not the boy's mom."

Beth pulled her hand away from his face. For a moment Cody thought she was going to slap him. She seemed to be thinking about it. Finally she put her hands on her hips and said, "No, I'm not his mother, may God rest her soul. But I'm someone who cares about him, which is more than I can say for you."

Before Coach Lathrop could retort, Cody's dad chimed in. "Mr. Lathrop, this conversation is now over. We've shared our concerns with you—and we will also share them with the organizers of the league. Meanwhile, there is still a tournament to be completed. We will speak with Cody about whether or not he should continue playing. But if he is cleared to play, you will not put him in harm's way again. Do you understand me on that?"

Coach Lathrop's face flushed. He appeared on the verge of a tirade, but after several suspense-filled seconds, he simply nodded and walked briskly away.

A few of the other parents who had gathered to watch the confrontation nodded their approval and patted Luke Martin on the back.

"You're doing the right thing," Goddard's father noted.

"Son," Cody's dad commanded when he saw him, "please get in the car. We're taking you to the emergency room right away to have your ribs X-rayed. And next time, you must tell me when you've been injured. I shouldn't have to hear it from Deke Porter after you've played a tournament game in such a condition."

"Chop," Cody muttered angrily to himself.

"You should thank him, not criticize him," Beth said. "He was really worried about you. He's a good friend. Besides, he didn't want to tell us at first when we asked him why you were running like you were hurt, but we bribed him with a milk shake. Every man has his price, you know."

"A milk shake, huh?" Cody said, smiling. "That sounds good."

Cody's dad offered him a grudging smile. "*After* the X-rays."

Cody uttered a deep sigh of relief when he heard the doctor's verdict—"Just a bruised rib—nothing broken."

Still, his dad held him out of the Saturday afternoon game, which the Rockies lost to the Plainsmen.

"Guess we just couldn't win without the dawg out there," Pork Chop said to Cody's dad after the game. "But it's all good. We beat Lincoln with Madison pitching. Brett got a no-hitter, for the first time in his life. I can almost die happy."

That night, just before he surrendered to sleep, Cody heard a pack of dogs barking underneath his bedroom window. He tried to shake the drowsiness from his head as he swung his legs over his bed. He walked silently to the window and opened the blinds.

A yawn turned to a smile as he looked down and saw Pork Chop, the Evans twins, and Doug Porter—heads tilted toward him—howling and barking at full volume.

"Good game, dawg!" Pork Chop shouted. "Way to put yourself out there for the team! You're crazier than I am! I've never, never seen anybody steal home before. That was fierce!"

"Thanks for the no-hitter," Brett added. "I never coulda done it without you!" With that, the foursome turned and sprinted to Doug's Camry. Doug left rubber in the Martin driveway before roaring away.

Cody slid carefully into his bed. He woke the next morning with a smile on his face. He wondered if it had been there all night.

He also woke up with a plan. He talked his dad into letting him play the final game of the tournament, which the Rockies entered without their head coach. Mr. McClintock had taken over, explaining to the team that Coach Lathrop decided it was "in the best interest of everyone involved" if he stepped aside.

The Rockies faced the Braves, who won a hard-fought 8–5 victory. Cody went two-for-four from the plate, with two bunt singles down the third base line. Pork Chop homered in his last at bat, sending a Guzman fastball at least thirty feet beyond the center-field fence, where it almost hit a white poodle.

The loss eliminated Grant from the tournament, but no one seemed to mind. The Brett Evans no-hitter was the talk of the tournament.

Murphy came to the final game and screamed himself hoarse from the Rockies' dugout. After the game, Brett tried to give his no-hitter game ball to Murph, who politely refused it.

"You earned that, so keep it," he said. "You guys already gave me the best gift I could imagine."

Chapter 6

Danger in High Places

With baseball season officially over, Cody took a week off from doing anything more athletic than watching ESPN.

But he couldn't stay on the couch long. He and Drew resumed their running, working up to an occasional eight-miler. And he finally kept a summer-long promise to Robyn that he would shoot hoops with her before high school started.

"Thanks for doing this, finally," Robyn said, "being my rebounder."

Cody caught Robyn's twenty-third consecutive free throw as it whispered through the net at the Grant Park outdoor court.

He smiled at her. "Technically, I think you have to miss before I can officially be called your rebounder."

"Well, let's do some catch-and-shoots next. I need help on those. My shot really needs work."

Cody shook his head. "Yeah, right. Is that what you told Alston this past basketball season?"

Robyn frowned. "He was mad about what I did, wasn't he?"

"Let's see, Hart. It's the heart of hoops season. Coach Clayton brings you into practice because Alston has been talking so much trash about what a scoring machine he is. He has you two play H-OR-S-E, and you smoke him on seven shots. You don't miss once. You don't even get one letter. How do you think a guy with an ego that big is going to feel?"

"Maybe he's going to realize his ego is bigger than his game. One needs to grow, the other needs to shrink."

"I think he's making some progress. Maturing a little."

With that, Cody fired a chest pass to Robyn as she backed up to the top of the key. Her shot hit the front of the rim and she slapped herself on the thigh. Cody retrieved the ball and passed it to her again. This time the ball rattled through.

"Still not right," she muttered.

"What? You have to swish every shot now?"

"Why not? Why not shoot for perfection?" Robyn moved to the right wing and banked in an eighteen-footer. "Dude, I can't wait for my high school career to start. I just have to make varsity my freshman year. Nobody's done that for, like, three years."

"I hope you do. Me, I'll be lucky to make the freshman team."

"I don't know, Cody. You have some skills. And you're the best stopper around. I like the way you play D."

Cody shrugged. "Thanks."

"But you know what I like even more?"

"Chocolate?"

"Ha, ha, ha. No, idiot. It's what you did for AJ Murphy. How you organized the baseball team to be there for him when he needed it most. It reminded me of how you stood up for Greta Hopkins this past year. You showed me something. More important, you've showed AJ and Greta something—God's love."

"I don't know about that."

"I do. You see, when I moved here in fourth grade, some kids made fun of me because of my glasses. I just wanted to cry. But then this skinny kid comes up and says, 'Come on, you guys—how would you feel if you wore glasses and you got treated this way?' Then this skinny kid introduces me to his friend Jill Keller, who becomes one of my best friends. That skinny kid made a difference for me. Now he's done it for other people, too."

Cody practiced a yo-yo pass, trying valiantly not to smile. "Man, I had forgotten all about that. That was a long time ago."

"I remember. It's not the kind of thing a girl forgets."

"For real?"

"For real. Take Greta, for example. I can promise you she won't forget what you did. Not in four years. Not in forty years."

Cody nodded. He bounced a pass to Robyn on the left baseline. She head faked and then swished a fifteen-foot jumper.

Smiling, she said, "Finally. That's more like it."

Luke Martin sat cross-legged on the floor, a disemboweled vacuum in front of him. To the left of the machine was a cone-shaped pile of dirt that looked like a giant gray anthill.

Uh-oh, Cody thought. *Dad's trying to fix something. This can't be good.*

He remembered the time in fifth grade when he came home to find his mom pacing the kitchen, wringing her hands. Dad was under the sink—so far under that Cody could see only his legs protruding from the cabinet.

"Sweetheart, can you hand me the pipe wrench?" Cody had heard his dad call. "I'll find that earring in no time."

"Heaven help us," Cody's mom had whispered as she handed over the wrench.

It had taken every towel in the Martin household to sop up the water that cascaded onto the kitchen floor when Cody's dad removed a section of pipe—without shutting off the water valves first.

Later, as Cody handed the heavy, dripping towels to his mom and she loaded them into the washing machine, she had told him, "I get so frightened when I see your dad with tools in his hands. I'm just thankful that we don't own any power tools."

Cody's dad looked up from the vacuum project. "Hey, Code, what's up? You okay?"

Cody sighed. "I guess so. I was just thinking back on the Murphy funeral. I mean, Murph was really surprised to see the whole team show up. I could tell he was glad we were there. But it brought back hard memories for me, about Mom. Memories I'm having a hard time shaking."

His dad nodded. "I was afraid that might happen. Nonetheless, you did the right thing."

"I know. I'm glad we were there for Murph. I can't imagine how tough it is for him. He's kind of quiet, and I don't know if he has any close friends here."

"Well, you were a good friend to him. I'm proud of you. I'm sorry I didn't tell you that before. Most kids who have gone through what you have would be thinking about themselves when that Dreaded Death Anniversary came up. But you reached out. You were unselfish. Just like your mom was. It must feel good to do what you did."

"Yeah, but—"

"But what?"

"I don't know if I can explain it, Dad."

"You can try."

"Well, I thought that if I could get through the, uh, anniversary, I would start to feel better about things. Like I had reached a goal or something. That I could have—I don't know—peace."

Cody's dad set down his screwdriver and popped to his feet. He put both hands on Cody's shoulders and studied his face. "Finding peace can take a long time. Sometimes I think I've found it, but then I start to think about what we lost, and I get angry all over again—confused, hopeless. They say grief is a process, but it's not a smooth process. Maybe you can relate?"

"Kind of, Dad. But what's bugging me most is that I still feel like I let her down."

"Let her down? No way, Son. Think of all you've accomplished this year. Shutting out East in football. Making the all-tournament team in basketball, winning your first race in track. And standing up for that poor girl—Gertrude, was it?"

Cody smiled. "Greta. Her name is Greta, Dad."

"Yeah, that's right. Standing up for her to those bullies at your school—that took courage. I know your mom is more proud of you for that than for any of the athletic stuff, or your straight-B average in school. Son, when I think about it all—the baseball no-hitter, your thoughtfulness, all of it—I don't understand how you can possibly say you let anyone down, especially your mom."

Cody felt a hot tear slide down his cheek. "But I couldn't say a word at her service. I wanted so bad to tell that churchful of people what an awesome person she is, but I knew I wouldn't be able to get three words out without breaking down. She did so much for me, and I just want to do something for her. To honor her, you know, just like the commandment says."

"Just a minute," his dad said, frowning thoughtfully. "I'll be right back."

Luke Martin disappeared up the stairs to his bedroom and returned with something cupped in his hands. "Here," he said, extending his hands to Cody.

Cody reached out to accept the small maroon velvet bag tied with a matching ribbon. He opened it. For a moment he was puzzled. "So, Dad, you're giving me a bag of rocks and dir—oh, hold on. Is this—"

His dad nodded. "Yes, Son. When your mom was . . . well, you know. I saved some of her ashes. Some for me. Some for you. On Saturday, August third, I drove to the park, where she and I used to picnic, and scattered them on her favorite hill. I thought you might want to do something, as well. I was waiting for the right time to give this to you. But with the tournament and the Murphy funeral and your injury—I admit, I kind of forgot for a while. I'm sorry."

Cody held the bag in his open palm. It was heavier than he expected. *It's more like stones and sand*, he thought. *I always figured the ashes were like the ones from a cigarette or a campfire.*

Swallowing hard, his dad said, "Anyway, Code, take some time. Think about what you'd like to do."

Cody nodded. "I will, Dad. But I think I already know."

Standing on a sidewalk in downtown Manitou Springs, Cody felt Blake's and Chop's eyes on him, studying him. Finally his teammate let out a long, slow whistle, like the kind a kid makes to mimic the sound of a bomb falling. "Dude, this is the craziest thing you've ever attempted. A fourteen-thousand-foot mountain, an eight-thousand-foot gain in elevation? I mean, whoa! But it's also the coolest thing."

Cody reached his arms high above his head and stretched. "Thanks, Chop. Mom loved Pikes Peak. Admired it. But she never got to the top. She wanted to hike it, but that never worked out. Then, when she first started feeling bad, we planned to drive to the top, on the Pikes Peak Highway. But she got nauseated less than halfway up. It was disappointing because she wanted to see that view. She would always say, 'You know, that panorama inspired the song "America the Beautiful."' And I'd go, 'Really? Cool.' Anyway, I know she'd approve."

"Yeah," Chop whispered.

"Now all I have to do is make it to the top. Man, I've never even run ten miles on a flat course. Don't know how I'm going to do thirteen up a mountain. But I have to try."

Blake walked over to Cody and draped his arm around his shoulder. "You sure you don't want company? I'm not in that great of shape, but—"

"Nah, thanks, B. I gotta do this alone. Besides, if I wouldn't let Drew Phelps come with me, what makes you think I'd even consider dragging your over-the-hill carcass along?"

Blake looked as if he were going to protest, but he stopped himself. "Okay, then. I'm gonna buy Chop dinner, maybe see a movie, and then we'll drive to the summit and see you there in about four and a half hours."

"I hope so," Cody said solemnly. "I sure hope so."

He took a deep breath, said his trademark "Help!" prayer, and began the third-of-a-mile trot that would take him to the head of Barr Trail. The bit of extra distance would make the run exactly thirteen miles. On the drive from Grant to Manitou, he had explained to Blake and Chop, "I have to do thirteen miles, because thirteen is supposedly an unlucky number. And Mom didn't believe in unlucky numbers. So when I run the distance and scatter her ashes at the top of the mountain, I think, finally, it will be the right tribute to her."

He felt the sports drink in the three water bottles on his running belt slosh as he headed up the wooden steps that marked the official beginning of Barr Trail.

Soon he came to a series of steep switchbacks that swung rhythmically back and forth. He used the end posts of a series of thick log fences to slingshot himself up each section of trail. Before long, the hum of Manitou traffic was behind him, and the only noises were the occasional chirp of a bird and the sound of his running shoes scuffing over dirt and gravel. He kept his eyes focused forward and slightly down, watching for the embedded rocks and baseball-bat-thick tree roots that Drew had warned him about.

A half hour into the run, he patted a pocket of his belt to ensure that his father's cell phone—and three energy bars—were still there. Then he slid his hand to a smaller pocket to check the small velvet bag with his mom's ashes.

At forty minutes Cody reached the Nose Rock, a huge piece of stone that looked as if it could serve as the nose for one of the guys on Mount Rushmore, if his current one fell off for some reason.

At the one-hour mark Cody reached French Creek, about four miles into the run, and began munching on the first energy bar. "If you wait until you're really hungry to eat," Drew had told him, "you've waited too long." The bar tasted like a shoe. *Except a shoe would probably have more flavor*, Cody thought. *But as long as it gives me energy, I guess I'll let the taste thing slide.*

As he trudged through Barr Camp, just past the halfway point, Cody felt a sense of panic begin to rise in him, starting in his ASICS-clad feet, then drifting upward like smoke to his gut, his heart. He was exhausted. He still had miles of steep, rocky ground to cover. And the air was getting thinner.

Breathing hard, Cody dialed his cell phone. He looked at his watch as he listened to the faraway, gurgling ring.

"B," he said when he heard Blake answer, "I'm doing okay. Already through Barr Camp. But you and Chop better make it about five hours, not four-point-five. I'm hurting a little, running out of gas."

"You gonna be okay? I'm concerned. Are your ribs starting to bother you again?" Blake's voice sounded as if it were coming from another world. A world inhabited by sane people who didn't embark on adventures for which they weren't remotely qualified.

"Nah, I'm okay and everything. Not hurt, only tired. This is just harder than I thought. Way harder. But if I slow down, I think I'll be all right."

"Good strategy. And you remembered to refill your water bottles at Barr Camp, right?"

Cody swallowed hard. "Uh—"

"Dude, if you're not too far beyond the camp, you need to get back there, okay? You don't want to be getting dehydrated at fourteen thousand feet!"

"B, you're right that I should go back. Sorry. I just forgot."

Cody clicked off the phone. "There's no way I'm going back," he muttered. "I can't go backward at this point. Besides, I still have almost a bottle and a half left. And, who knows, maybe it'll rain."

As Cody climbed toward the A-frame lean-to that marked the ten-mile point of his journey, he encountered a series of switchbacks again. They seemed endless. Every time he crested one of them, hoping for a section of level ground, he rounded a corner, only to find another steep climb ahead, taunting him. The increasingly rocky terrain added to his woes. His feet ached from traversing the sharp, unforgiving rocks that jutted from the trail.

He guessed he was about a mile from the A-frame when, for the first time, he found himself gasping desperately for breath. Each time he inhaled, it was like taking a gulp from a canteen—and finding it held only a drop of water.

Finally he saw the A-frame, perched at the edge of Dismal Forest, so named because it was littered with bristlecone pine trees that had been struck by lightning.

Well, Cody thought, trying to reassure himself, *at least I haven't seen any lightning. I might suffocate, but at least I won't get fried by a lightning bolt.*

As he left Dismal Forest behind, he noticed light fog settling in around him. *No problem*, he told himself. *It's windy. That'll blow this stuff away.*

However, just as he dribbled the last few drops of water bottle number two into his mouth, he found himself engulfed in fog so thick that he had to stop. It reminded him of when he took a hot shower after a workout and filled his small bathroom with so much steam that he had to feel his way to find the sink or the towel rack.

Cody narrowed his eyes, straining to see the trail ahead of him—and which way it would bend and climb next. Carefully he began walking in what he felt was the right direction. He knew he had failed when his right foot slid off some scree at the trail's edge and he tumbled downward. He felt himself roll three times before a large boulder, which he smacked into with his left side, stopped him.

Hmmm, he thought grimly. *And here I thought my bruised ribs were all healed. Apparently not. Or maybe it's "not anymore."*

He rose slowly to his feet. He reached for his third water bottle—and felt cold panic slither up his spine when he discovered it wasn't there. He would have swallowed hard, but he couldn't muster up enough saliva.

"This is not good," he admitted aloud, gasping. *I still have three miles to go*, he thought, *and I'm getting dehydrated. Man, I can't believe it. Here I am, trying to carry Mom's ashes to the top of the mountain, and I just might die in the process. That would be just too—What was the word? Ironic.* "Yeah," he whispered hoarsely. "Ironic."

Cody grabbed his cell phone. Holding it inches from his face, he struggled to discern the numbers. He wasn't sure if it was due to fog or fatigue. He slid his fingers along the keypad, dialing by feel more than sight. Pressing the phone to his ear, he waited. He heard nothing. *Maybe I can't get a signal*, he reasoned. *Or maybe I broke the phone when I fell. Oh well, at least there's someone I can always connect with.*

"God," he pleaded, "I'm scared. I admit it. Please help me. I know I need to go up, but I'm not sure where up is."

He waited for a few moments, leaning into the wind and staring hard at the milky fog in front of him. For a moment he caught a glimpse of a sliver of trail. Energized, he began walking again. Soon his eyes fell upon a trail marker.

Cool, he thought. *The marker will point the direction of the trail and maybe tell me how far I have to go. Thank you, Lord!*

He reached the marker and stopped, waiting for his eyes to focus. He heard himself laughing grimly as he read the brief tribute to G. Inestine Roberts, who had died near this spot during her fourteenth ascent of the peak. *Well*, he told himself, *that's encouraging.*

He prayed again, *Oh, Lord, and to think some people don't believe you have a sense of humor! But if it's all the same to you, I really don't want to meet the same fate as G. Inestine Roberts, please.*

Cody left the Roberts memorial behind him, his hope growing as he realized he could now at least make out small portions of trail ten to fifteen feet in front of him. He knew he was in the bleak, barren landscape above timberline now, and this brought him another encouraging realization—*At least if I wander off the trail, I won't smack into any trees.*

Cody tried to laugh but found he couldn't. He inhaled deeply and suddenly found himself coughing. *Okay*, he thought, assessing the situation, *there is no discernible oxygen here. And I can barely see where I'm going. And I'm dehydrated and have nothing to drink.*

The word *drink* flipped a switch in his mind, and he realized that he did have another energy bar. "At least that's something," he gasped. He began eagerly shucking the wrapper off the bar.

When he took his first bite of the bland rectangle, he learned something he hadn't known before—you can chew food all you want, but you can't swallow it when your mouth is as dry as dust.

As he stuffed the energy bar back into his waist pack, Cody chuckled to himself. "This will be a funny story, if I live to tell it," he whispered.

Eventually the fog began to thin out a bit more, just enough for him to realize he had reached the sixteen Golden Stairs, a brutally steep series of thirty-two staircase-like switchbacks. *I don't know why they call 'em sixteen Golden Stairs when there are thirty-two of them*, he thought. *Maybe people can't do math very well up here in the thin air.*

As he began his assault of the first section of "stairs," Cody found that his quadriceps ached so badly that he had to concentrate on each step. *Left foot*, he would tell himself. *Okay, now right foot—*

He figured he was halfway up the stairs when he saw faint light above him, straining to break through the clouds. He wasn't sure if it was actually sunlight or just a hallucination caused by exhaustion, but he trudged toward it nonetheless.

Cody felt his legs buckle a bit and began to use the "four-wheel drive" technique that Drew had taught him. He placed a hand on each knee and pushed his way up the remaining Golden Steps. He could see now that the light was no illusion. He was leaving the clouds behind him. Sunlight was ahead.

When he reached the long final slope leading to the summit, 14,110 feet above sea level, Cody began to run again, bounding up the trail with long, ground-gobbling strides.

He reached the top and sank immediately to his knees. *Lord,* he said, *I have to admit, I just hit my knees from exhaustion, not religious devotion, but since I'm down here—Thank you. Thank you. Thank you!"*

He stood and began to search for a place to scatter his mother's ashes. A marmot peeked around a rock, chirping cheerfully at him. Cody smiled and reached into his waist pack. He found the energy bar and lobbed it to the animal. The marmot fell silent in mid-chirp and scurried away.

"The way those things taste, I'd be afraid, too, little fella," Cody said, laughing. "But maybe you'll get brave and try it later."

He slowly turned his body 360 degrees. His eyes immediately found the right spot, to the right of the Summit House. He walked to it, alternately gazing in wonder at the cloud cover below and the bright sunlight above. Then he carefully opened the bag and poured its contents into his cupped right hand. He felt a gust of wind kick up behind him, and he held his hand high, letting the breeze take the ashes. Then he tossed the remaining heavier "stones."

"Goodbye, Mom," he said quietly. "You made it to the top. Finally. And I want you to know that to me, you'll always be the best mom a kid could have. Thank you for everything you did for me. And that's a big 'everything.'"

Beth had insisted on slipping Cody a twenty-dollar bill just before he left the house. He thought it a stupid idea at the time, but now, sipping on a bottle of sports drink he purchased in the Summit House, the restaurant and tourist gift shop atop the Peak, he was grateful for her foresight. One of the paramedics stationed at the top of the mountain told Cody that the Pikes Peak Highway was closed due to the fog, so Blake wouldn't be able to pick him up.

"You can either ride the cog railway down the mountain, or I'll take you when I get off work, but that's a few hours from now," the paramedic told him.

Cody began sorting the change from the twenty dollars. "Well," he said slowly, "can I get a one-way cog ticket and buy a few famous Summit House donuts for a friend of mine for eighteen bucks?"

The paramedic smiled. "Yeah. You should be able to cover that."

"Good," Cody said, smiling back. "This friend, I'm sure he's disappointed right now. I think the main reason he offered to come along with the guy who was supposed to pick me up was to taste one of the legendary high-altitude donuts."

Epilogue

Under normal circum-
stances, the robust hugs
Cody received from Blake and
Pork Chop at the cog railway station would have
made him feel awkward. But he found he was too
tired to care.

"So," Blake said as Cody slid into the backseat of
his car and lay down, "were you scared when you got
lost in the clouds up there?"

Cody raised his head. "Uh, *yeah!*"

"Well," Blake said, "we were praying for you."

"We?"

Pork Chop bit into his third donut, pausing a
moment to savor it. "Yeah, we. I'm allowed to pray,

dawg. Just because I'm not a church boy like you doesn't mean I don't pray. My people, you know, we're very spiritual."

Cody let his head fall back onto the seat. "Some more than others, I guess."

"Anyway," Pork Chop said, apparently ignoring the jab, "thanks for the donuts. Man, these boys are tasty."

"Well, thank you for praying for me. It worked. Hey, Blake?"

"Yeah?"

"You know what was weird about today? When I couldn't see where I was going, it was so hopeless. I felt like I would never see light again. But when I finally climbed above the clouds and left them below me, there was the sun, shining just like always."

"Yeah," Pork Chop said, puzzled, "the sun does tend to shine. That's kinda what it does."

Blake chuckled. "True enough, Chop, but I think Mr. Martin has a deeper point here."

"Yeah," Cody said. "I think I do, anyway. See, when I got to the top, I started thinking about how high I was up on the mountain when the fog first engulfed me. I think it was around ten thousand feet. And I didn't get above it till near the summit, at above fourteen thousand. So I realized that at the time when I first got lost in the fog, I was actually closer to the sun than I've ever been in life."

"Mmm-hmm," Blake said. "Maybe closer to the Son, S–O–N, too, eh?"

"Yeah," Cody said quietly. He listened for a few moments to the hum of the tires on the highway. Then, surprised that Chop hadn't weighed in on the subject, he asked, "Chop, you okay? I don't even hear eating."

"The donuts are all gone, my brother. I'm just thinking right now."

"About what?"

"About what you said. About the sun being close, even when you felt like it was far away. That's kinda cool."

Cody smiled and closed his eyes. "Yeah," he said, "it *is* cool."

As the miles rolled by underneath, Cody felt fatigue wrapping itself around him. He tried to resist it, thinking of how high school would start in two weeks, football camp in just one. But sleep was inevitable. There was time for only one more quick prayer.

Father God, I don't know what's ahead for me this year. I don't know if I can compete in high school sports. I don't know if I can pass high school classes. I don't know how I'll handle it if Dad and Beth decide to get married or something. But whatever the future brings, help me to remember today. How you can't get too discouraged by the clouds that surround you. How you gotta keep thinking of what's shining above 'em. Amen.

SPIRIT
OF THE
GAME

It's not how hard you play, it's who you play for!

GOAL LINE STAND

BY TODD HAFER

zonderkidz

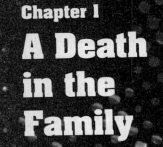

Chapter 1
A Death in the Family

As Cody lay on the field, his mind drifted back to the day of his mom's funeral.

Cody squirmed in the front pew of Crossroads Community Church, trying to wriggle his way into a comfortable position. He sighed heavily and twisted around to study the scene behind him. He felt dozens of eyes lock on him, then nervously dart away. Except for those of Mrs. Adams, his grade school Sunday school teacher, who gazed at him lovingly. She was five rows back, but Cody could see that her eyes were red and puffy from crying. He tried to smile at her and then turned around. He usually sat in the back of church—the very back, in one of the metal folding chairs lined against the rear wall of the sanctuary.

"The best seats in the house," Cody always called them. They allowed him to slip out to the restroom or the foyer without disapproving stares from his mom and dad—or that busybody Mrs. Underwood. And, during the occasional Sunday when he couldn't follow Pastor Taylor's sermon, he could pass the time by counting bald spots, then figuring the percentage of follically-impaired men in the congregation. The last time he counted, 23 percent of the Crossroads men were Missing Hair Club candidates.

The percentage was slightly higher if you counted Mr. Sanders, whose sandy toupee always rested atop his head at a jaunty angle, like a dozing badger.

On the rare Sundays when Pork Chop accompanied Cody to church, the duo would slip out to the foyer during the special music—which usually wasn't very special at Crossroads—and feast on the remaining donuts on the refreshment table.

The good donuts, the ones filled with jelly or crowned with multi-colored sprinkles, were always gone, plucked by those devoted enough to come to the early service. But the remainder, the glazed ones with watery icing beading on them like perspiration, were better than nothing.

"Donuts—at church!?" Chop said once while sucking glaze off his fingers with loud smacks. "Now that's a heavenly idea! It's almost worth coming to church every Sunday. Almost."

Cody leaned forward and rested his elbows on his knees. Pork Chop was in church again today, but there would be no joking. Chop sat three rows behind Cody, sporting a too tight suit and sandwiched between his father and his mammoth half brother, Doug.

Cody had begged his dad to let Pork Chop sit by him, but had been informed that such an arrangement wasn't "proper funeral protocol."

Cody was bookended by his dad and Gram Martin, his paternal grandmother. Cody looked at Gram, who looked older, plumper, and sadder than the last time he saw her, even though it was just two weeks ago. She was sniffling quietly and dabbing at her eyes with a tattered lavender tissue. It was no secret that Cody's mom and Gram Martin didn't get along, but the grief seemed genuine.

Or maybe it's regret, Cody thought. Maybe Gram is thinking of all the shouting matches she and Mom got into and feeling guilty.

He turned his attention from his grandmother to the coffin at the front of the church, just below the pulpit.

I can't believe my mom's in there, *he thought,
shaking his head. But it was true. He saw her in
there only twelve hours ago. He had waited
patiently in the foyer, pawing at the carpet with his
foot as he listened to the choir practice "Amazing
Grace," which was his mom's favorite hymn during the final weeks of her life. The choir sounded
somber, but pretty good—better than he had heard
in a long time.*

*When the singing stopped, Ben Woods, of Woods
Family Funeral Home, approached Cody. "You can
see her now, if you wish," Ben said, with a calmness
and compassion that Cody guessed had taken years
to perfect.*

*Wish. The word floated through his mind. I wish
this whole thing wasn't real, he thought. I wish I were
anywhere but here. I wish Mom weren't lying dead in
a giant box.*

*Cody felt Ben's fingers touch his elbow. "Would you
like me to get your father, Cody, so you can go in
together? He's in the pastor's office."*

*"No," Cody said, surprised at how hard it was to
make a sound. "I kinda need to do this alone."*

*Ben nodded and led Cody to the front of the sanc-
tuary. With practiced ease, he raised the top portion
of a two-piece lid and locked it into position.*

"I will give you as long as you need," he said. "I'll close the sanctuary door behind me when I exit, to give you some privacy. Just come and find me when you're ready. And, Cody, I am very sorry for your loss."

Cody felt his head nodding. He had waited until he heard the door latch click before he allowed himself to look at her.

They had done her hair. Wispy honey-colored bangs rested on her forehead, the ends nearly touching her thin eyebrows. Cody noted the thick makeup layered on her face, like frosting on a cake. It reminded him of the makeup the high school thespians wore for their spring musicals.

He heard himself exhale sadly. When she was alive, Linda Martin rarely wore makeup. She used to joke that she wanted people to see a few lines on her face. "Maybe then they'll let me teach adult Sunday school—not just work the nursery," she would say.

Cody's dad had a different take. "You don't need makeup, Lin," he told her regularly. "Why cover up perfection?"

But the folks at Woods Family Funeral Home had covered up plenty. Cody remembered relatives talking about funerals from time to time. He recalled snippets like, "He looked so natural," and "She looked so peaceful lying there in the coffin."

But his mom didn't look natural or at peace. She looked empty. He studied her face. Slowly, tentatively, he raised his left hand. It floated toward her, as if under a power not his own.

He let his fingertips rest for a moment on her cheek. The skin felt cool, lifeless. More like rubber than human flesh. He drew his hand back.

I hope I forget how that felt, *he thought.* That's not how I want to remember things.

"Bye, Mom," *he whispered.* "And thank you. Thank you for everything you did. The meals—the laundry—the help with homework. Coming to my games. I wish I had been more grateful. I'll try to say something about you tomorrow, but I'm not sure I can. If I can't, I hope you'll understand. And I hope that, somehow, you know that I'll always love you. Please, God, let there be some way for her to know that—and to know how much I miss her already."

He felt his throat tighten. He turned toward the exit, gazing at the stained glass windows as he walked down the rust-colored carpet that ran down the center of the sanctuary. The last window depicted a sunrise scene, with a white dove gliding across the morning sky. Inscribed above a golden rising sun were the words, I AM THE RESURRECTION AND THE LIFE.

Before he opened the door leading to the foyer, Cody let his eyes move from the words to the church's high ceiling. "Yeah," he whispered solemnly, hopefully. "The life."

Cody felt himself being led to the sideline, Brett Evans under his left arm, Pork Chop under his right. Both were five foot eight, two inches taller than he was, so his feet glided across the short-cropped grass as they left the field. It felt almost like walking on air. He looked into the stands and saw about half the home crowd standing, rendering a polite smattering of applause. He searched for his dad's face, but knew he wouldn't find it.

This is gonna be just like seventh grade ball, he thought. *He's gonna keep blowing off games 'til the season's over. Only now I won't have Mom in the stands. I could always count on her. Now I don't have anybody.*

Pork Chop helped Cody lower himself to the bench. "It was Tucker who ear-holed you, right, Code?" he asked.

"Either him or a Mack truck."

"Well, just watch what happens next. It's gonna be payback time next time we're on defense. I'm gonna hit him so hard that it'll knock the taste out of his mouth."

"Chop—"

"Don't argue with me, my brother. Just chill and watch the fun. We're losing by twenty anyway. I gotta do something to keep myself motivated."

Cody started to protest and then shrugged his shoulders, which brought the stabbing pain back again.

Coach Smith kept him out of the game's final four minutes, during which Clay scored again on the QB sweep. On that play, Pork Chop chased down Tucker from behind and rode him to the ground, even though it was obvious that he was a blocker, not the ball carrier. After the referee raised both hands to the sky, signaling the TD, Chop smacked his palms against the sides of his helmet, feigning anger at himself for being duped. Then he extended a thick forearm to Tucker and jerked him to his feet.

Tucker stood, wobbly and disoriented. It reminded Cody of the newborn scene in *Bambi*. The fullback got off the field just in time to avoid Central's receiving an offside penalty on the ensuing kickoff.

By the Monday morning following the Central game, the pain in Cody's neck had faded. The pain in his heart, however, still burned. He smiled anyway.

He smiled at Coach Smith, who saw him in the hallway at school and asked, "You doin' okay, Code?"

He smiled at Robyn Hart, his friend since fourth grade, when she told him, "Good game on Saturday."

And he smiled at Kris Knight, the new student that Principal Prentiss introduced him to in the school office before first hour.

This is weird, Cody thought. *You don't even have to be happy to smile. Just like you don't have to be mean to play football. You just have to act like it, and I guess no one knows the difference.*

"Mr. Knight," Mr. Prentiss was saying, "welcome to the eighth grade at Grant Middle School. This is Cody Martin. This is his second year as one of our orientation mentors. He will be accompanying you to most of your classes, as your schedules are almost identical. He will help you find your classrooms, the cafeteria, and whatnot."

"Yeah," Cody said, injecting artificial happiness into his voice, "we have great whatnot here at Grant."

Mr. Prentiss unleashed a laugh that was as fake as Mr. Sanders's toupee.

As they headed toward first-period PE, Cody tried to think of a conversation starter. "So," he said finally to his "mentee," as Mr. Prentiss called them, "you do any sports back at your old school?"

Knight had arms like broomsticks, and Cody noticed that his feet splayed out at 45-degree angles when he walked. It was as if his left foot and right foot disagreed on which direction their owner should be going. Still, you had to ask. Polite conversation— that's what Dad and Mr. Prentiss called it.

Knight cleared his throat. "Nah, I'm not really into sports. I mean, I like them and everything, but I have asthma. I played in the pep band, though. Clarinet."

Cody nodded. "That's cool." He saw Knight looking at his white football jersey, which bore a faded blue number 7. John Elway's number.

Cody heard the throat clear again. It sounded like a dirt bike engine revving. "You must play, huh, Cody?"

"Yeah, I can't remember a time when I wasn't playing something. T-ball. Y-league hoops. Pop Warner football. Age-group track meets. You name it."

"That's cool," Knight said, unconvincingly.

They entered the gym and sat together on the first row of wooden bleachers. Ten boys, divided into shirts and skins, were playing full-court basketball. Another seven or eight sat on the bleachers near Cody and Knight, awaiting their turn.

Coach Smith, who taught PE in addition to coaching football and wrestling, paced the sideline, wearing a pained expression on his face.

"Come on, ladies," he chided, his voice weary and sandpaper-rough from the past weekend's game, "this is physical education. So let's get physical. Sewing class is third hour. Porter, if Alston beats your entire team down the court for one more uncontested layup, you knuckleheads are doing push-ups until your arms fall off!"

"Who's Porter?" Knight whispered loudly. "Is he that big dude?"

"Yeah," Cody said with a laugh, "the one who's sweatin' so much he looks like he's been dipped in baby oil. That's Pork Chop."

"Pork Chop?"

"Yeah. See, when he was a baby and cutting teeth, his dad used to give him pork chop bones to gnaw on. Drove his mom crazy, from what I've heard. Anyway, that's where the nickname comes from. His real name's Deke."

"That's his real name? What's it short for?"

"It's short for nothing. Just Deke."

Knight nodded. "What should I call him?"

"Well, Chop always says, 'Call me anything—just don't call me late for dinner!'"

Knight laughed politely.

Cody leaned back, resting his elbows on the second tier of bleachers. "I probably should tell you one thing about Chop," he said. "You probably notice that he's got quite a tan."

Knight nodded again.

"Well, his dad's white. His mom was black. Still is, I guess. She bounced a couple years ago. See, we don't have a lot of, uh, African-Americans in this part of Colorado. It was hard for Chop's mom. It's been hard for him too. I've been with him when people have driven by and called him—well, you know. You should see his eyes when it happens. I mean, he's a tough guy, but when people say stuff like that, racial stuff—"

"People still do that? In Colorado?"

"People still do that. And worse. Anyway, he can be a bit sensitive about the subject. Just so you know. But don't get the wrong idea. He's cool. He has a great sense of humor. Funniest guy in the school, as far as I'm concerned."

"So, you guys are friends?"

"Best friends." Cody felt his voice cracking as he said the words. He hoped Kris Knight didn't notice.

They turned their attention back to the game. They watched Pork Chop grab a rebound, swinging his elbows viciously from side to side as two opposing players tried to steal the ball from him. "Get offa me!" he snarled.

"Watch the 'bows, Chop," Coach Smith snapped.

"Wow," Knight said. "I wouldn't want Pork Chop mad at me."

Cody whistled through his teeth. "No," he said, "you sure wouldn't."

After one of Pork Chop's teammates shot an air ball from the free throw line, the shirts team gained control of the ball and launched a fast break. Their point guard drove down the middle of the court, stopped abruptly at the top of the key, and lofted a jump shot that slid through the net without even grazing the rim.

"Wow," Knight said, "who's that guy? He's good!"

Cody watched Terry Alston stand and admire his shot for a moment, then turn and lope downcourt with smooth, easy strides.

"That's Alston," he said. "Best athlete in the whole school. Just ask him. He transferred here from a private school in the Springs—Colorado Springs. He says basketball's his best sport. And, from what I've seen in gym class so far, he's probably right. We should be pretty good this year. We'll have a new coach. It should be fun."

Softcover 0-310-70669-6

Available now at your local bookstore!

zonderkidz

**Author Todd Hafer brings you
more sports action with
Spirit of the Game sports fiction!**

Cody's Varsity Rush

Written by Todd Hafer
Softcover 0-310-70794-3

Three-Point Play

Written by Todd Hafer
Softcover 0-310-70795-1

Available now at your local bookstore!

zonderkidz

zonder**kidz**.

We want to hear from you. Please send your comments
about this book to us in care of zreview@zondervan.com. Thank you.

Grand Rapids, MI 49530
www.zonderkidz.com